The Other Alexander

MARGARITA LIBERAKI

The Other Alexander

Translated by
Willis Barnstone and Elli Tzalopoulou Barnstone

AIORA

Original title: *Ο άλλος Αλέξανδρος*

© Margarita Liberaki 1950
© Kastaniotis Editions S.A. 1995
© for this edition, Aiora Press 2021

This translation was first published by Noonday Press, New York, in 1959.
First edition by Aiora Press, June 2021
Reprinted June 2023

ISBN: 978-618-5369-39-2

AIORA PRESS
11 Mavromichali St.
Athens 10679 – Greece
tel: +30 210 3839000
www.aiorabooks.com

CONTENTS

CHAPTER 1

"At bottom you may be innocent, but deeper still you are diabolical."

That is what my father told me, shaking with laughter; whereas my mother liked to say how I was little once, just a tot, tinier than a big bird, and she suckled me. When I grew a bit and we passed by the cemetery and I would question her, she said this was the dwelling place of deer, so that I wouldn't be frightened, and also because I loved deer, having seen a photograph of them in a zoology textbook.

Nor was it right for my father to have said such a thing just as I was eagerly announcing my friend's engagement. I said I didn't know his fiancée personally, but surely she was blond and full-breasted.

It was curious that I hadn't even laid eyes on her, for he and I were great friends and our relationship was out of the ordinary. We saw each other almost every evening to smoke and read together. He played the piano. His way was to start with scales to loosen up his fingers, and then after an hour of classical music, he would improvise. At midnight his musical gift blossomed, filling you with wonder. I can say that never before had I so relished music. Was it his way of surrendering himself to the piano, or was it the late summer evenings and our friendship which was so out of the ordinary? We lit the lamp. He seldom got more than a puff from his cigarette, forgetting it in the ash-tray where it burnt out.

He had not even mentioned his engagement. Yet we had discussed women often, and very freely, because every woman has her manner and special charm. Some close their eyes while others leave them open and the pitch of their voices differs, and you cannot say you know a woman if you haven't slept with her. These things made us laugh. We drank a little and then elaborated on the details. My friend had once told me my soul was innocent, but that I was attracted by corruption. This is far different from the scathing remarks my father had made about my innocence.

"But you also know how to adapt yourself to corruption," my friend added.

The truth is that I can adapt myself to anything. Throw me in prison, and I will adjust to it; and if you leave me on a deserted island, I will learn its life, that is, I will learn to like it. Because I like everything and nothing really makes me unhappy. Perhaps I might suffer at the beginning, but later on I would get used to it. And those who so lightheartedly made me suffer would later be more unhappy than I, and perhaps still are today. But that is a different question. You never know with women because they don't know themselves.

And so, like clay, I fit the mold of every situation, and I have never known what is called "lack of appetite." I might say that on certain sad occasions, I was rather ashamed of my appetite because it is something you cannot hide. Not so much the quantity you consume but the manner of eating betrays you. And this greed becomes obvious with the first spoonful you bring to your mouth and in the way you lift your fork.

At my grandmother's death, for example, I was not able to conceal my hunger. After the funeral, although you should sip the broth leaving the meat untouched, when the boiled meat was served I nearly devoured it all. And this is how you should act when you claim to follow the general rather than the immediate course of events—to behave as if it were your neighbor's grandmother who died, so that your life, even in its petty troubles, may on the whole remain calm and unaltered—just as the ocean is the same in all its moments: here there is calm and there tempest; and when there is tempest here, there is calm somewhere else. Only its parts change, not the whole. The ocean is always the same with itself. And only man in his foolishness sees it differently.

So I can say with conviction that we were very close friends and that for almost everything he asked my advice. I was proud because he who had such a warm and direct nature, who played the piano so beautifully, had chosen me as his friend. Intuitively he knew what I was worth. And I, on the other hand, being of an instinctive and straightforward temperament, had chosen him, and the personality of one widened the personality of the other. In our way we multiplied ourselves, trying to find and extract the essence from things and books, to squeeze out the juice as one does from a lemon. Above all we looked for this essence in poetry, but also in algebra and geometrical shapes; for rational books also contain a deeper core for those who are willing to search it out.

We saw in each other's eyes our own worth and intelligence. He admired me and I admired him.

He was nevertheless thin as a stick, and could not but have chosen a full woman with rich breasts. "Tomorrow I'm getting engaged," he said to me one evening, as midnight neared and his musical self was widening from moment to moment. He never mentioned anything before or after that. After quickly inhaling his cigarette, he continued playing and I did not have the time to say anything. When we parted that night, we made no comment, but avoided each other's eyes.

After my father said his bit of nastiness, he began to laugh. He always laughed loudly and sonorously as if his laughter had its source in his belly, or rather in his legs, and passed through his body like an electric current and shook it. But his eyes did not laugh. And whenever he laughed with grave eyes, I was frightened. I curled up inside myself. I became a spool of thread, but I stood up very straight and pretended that I didn't care. I even laughed myself. Then my father stopped short and ordered coffee. He told me, "Go tell them to prepare some coffee for me." His way annoyed me and wounded my pride. I repeat it was his manner; for I would not even mind polishing anybody's shoes, if I were asked in a nice way. On the contrary, ever since I was small, I liked to clean the shoes of my brothers and school friends. They teased me about it. They considered it a lack of self-respect, but since I liked doing it, I polished and whistled.

My father's manner was unbearable, tyrannical. And he never felt any kind of shame for his life, although he should have. He was extremely severe about other people's petty mistakes; only with my sister Aglaia—or rather with my two sisters Aglaia—was he always lenient. How I happened to have two sisters of the same name I shall explain in detail, without stressing what shame Father should have felt about his life, nor restricting myself by the order of events in time. For events come by themselves, tumble on each other topsy-turvy. And anyway, every life is similar to every other, just as in the ocean every wave is alike, despite the difference of height or impulse.

Did I meet her at the ocean or at the Saronic gulf? I remember only the day, a Tuesday, and its texture. The day was hot and then overtaken by cold wind. But if I were to judge by the haze which suddenly rose from the sea and became an immovable cloud above our heads, I would say it was the ocean.

During all that period, the haze either thickened or thinned, and so with my ideas and feelings. Especially one day—on the same shore, exactly at the turning point where the road curved uphill to the village and you lost sight of the sea—one day when I felt emptied of ideas and sentiments and began to laugh with wild joy, a sea-storm broke loose. I was still laughing when I reached the village named for Saint Peter and famous for its Benedictine. Though I swear I started laughing before taking a sip. For as I said, my laughter began on the shore. At the inn, when I found myself face to face with her at the same table, the laughter froze on my lips. Then she started to laugh, like a cat—if cats ever laughed.

Sharp teeth and small ears. And her hands caressed invisible shapes in the air. This caressing had already attracted my attention at the shore. Her eyes were feline, gold-yellow with spots, and her body was supple, but without obviously furtive movements. On the contrary her step, as well as the movement of her shoulders, which follows in beat, was full of frankness. Her rhythm was entirely sincere. And if I were to liken her to an animal, I would say she was like a small colt, because of her swiftness and her desire to leap up and run. She was hasty and in continual movement and all this for nothing; for in front of the ocean her haste was without meaning and she was small as a flea, not to speak of her tiny bathing suit, speckled with minute designs of crabs, clams and little fish.

She spoke first—that also I can swear. I hadn't shown the least disposition for conversation. As it was afternoon and the beach deserted, I sat almost hidden between a rock and a rowboat drawn up on the sand. First I saw her shoes, green sandals, just a green strap to be exact. And then a white rag which must have been her dress. She was swimming. The amusing thing was that when she came out of the water, thinking herself alone, she began to behave as if she were alone. She made believe she was running, but didn't run, and lifted her head with infinite gratitude. She caressed the unseen shapes — I'm not exaggerating—and made other movements which people perform only in their privacy, as for instance when she raised her arm and looked at it, rubbing it as though something had pricked her, and then kissed it.

Her self-admiration in front of the sea was something which she would never forgive my seeing, and it always stood between us as a barrier—there are things which remain unsaid and unconfessed, and of course everybody has a right to his secret thoughts and movements which make up his character and differentiate him from other people. This is the beginning of character, much more than a bent towards mathematics or history. My friend and I had discussed this question and we made a point of observing the way passers-by in the streets blew their noses.

That evening, in her usual haste, she took off her clothes in front of me so quickly that I believed her dress to have been an illusion. She preferred the lights off, but during the whole time, it was as if she felt nothing. Then we began to talk about the proprietress of the inn and the way she cooked sauces. It must have been at the ocean, for now I remember there was a storm that same night and the weather was quite cold in the morning, things not likely to happen in the Saronic gulf in mid-July. The coast-line was very precipitous and wild, and the horizon was lost, whereas from the Saronic gulf you can see the islands opposite. Nor should I confuse her with the woman of the Saronic, who groaned during the whole time, who never hurried for anything, whose neck was tender as a calf's. But both here and there were sea gulls screeching across the sky. Once—though hard to believe—I was a baby and cried in my swaddling bands and suckled at set hours and then began to eat a bit from each food and to tell wheat from the plane tree, heat from cold; and then I began to know my brothers and sisters, a difficult and confusing task, since my father had two families.

I was never late at table, which pleased my father, although he did not know, he declared, whether this was due to my respect for tradition or to an ironical compliance. "Silent revolutionaries are the most dangerous ones," he grumbled, and his glance weighed on the broad shoulders of my brother Grigori, who, with his open temperament, could not help but cry out whatever he was doing. He even boasted of more than he had done. He had mild eyes and shoulders upon which Father's look could easily lean and rest.

My brother Grigori even said that he had killed. But in the family we did not believe him or pretended not to; first because of his character; and secondly if he had really killed, he did so for political reasons when murder is not exactly murder, especially if one manages to forget the human flesh and how blood spurts from a gaping wound. More-over it was the fault of our times, for at another moment with such eyes Grigori would not have killed and might even have taken to embroidery. We say all this, presupposing he *had* murdered, which is very doubtful if one remembers my brother's mania to boast of his evil deeds and to hide the good ones.

My mother broke into laughter the evening Grigori told the story of the killing, in every detail, and she interrupted him to put in her word: Grigori told white lies, she said, ever since he was a small child—tall tales and nonsense; he told how he cracked the heads of his classmates during recess, how he strangled his opponents while wrestling. Actually he had only inflicted scratches and very slight bruises.

"Furthermore you had such thin little legs," she added, and then Grigori insisted on the murder, displaying his legs which had gotten much stronger in the meantime.

"I do not understand the sacrifice of getting myself killed," he said, "but the sacrifice of killing others I understand very well."

Mother then diverted the conversation, saying that he was not careful enough and dirtied his pants. Grigori chuckled about the girls he had led to the forest, young schoolgirls, but willing, and then Mother opened her eyes wide and looked at him in wonder, because Mother, despite her several childbirths, had the eyes of a virgin: she would never understand until her death. All these things gave her a vague unrest and she didn't know what to do. Then she turned to the cares of the house, which can well absorb a woman if she keeps up with the supply of salt and sugar and how much of each food is required for cooking a meal.

But the thing which my father despised was that whenever I had a chance to, I lay down and closed my eyes.

"Get up Alexander!"

My eyes opened; and unaccustomed to the light, I saw rhinoceros and wide crocodile mouths; or I remained motionless and felt my father's breath on my neck. At other times I decided to speak up for the right of each man to lie down with his eyes closed.

"Then you should go to your room," shouted my father. "In my presence it is unbecoming." Out of pure hypocrisy he was very attentive to whatever was dignified or unbecoming.

"Since he owns both the land and the undersoil why do you speak back to him?" said Phokion, my third brother, the only one who helped Father in the mines—the only one from this family— although he did not have our father's flair for finding the metal. Father found the precious veins just as a hunting dog finds the wounded bird, and he was unique as an organizer, knowing how to keep prestige with the workers. Towards his workers he had a goodness from high up, just like those people who take care not to tread on ant hills. He gave pensions to their widows and orphans, a thing well known in the district. Yet, as soon as the days became chilly, flocks of crows passed overhead, whole armies, especially towards twilight after vespers. A shiver ran through the fields.

Father calls me his unworthy son because I neither find the veins of metal nor behave as one should towards the workers and their widows. And Grigori calls me his unworthy brother because I've never killed and because I am sensitive to the sight of ruins and of blood. They both agree that all this is due to my idleness and to the fact that I lie down and close my eyes at high noon.

CHAPTER 2

"I don't see what my friend's engagement has to do with my being innocent or diabolical," I cried. I was angry and beside myself.

"Then how do you explain your curiosity to know the fiancée?" my father began. He laughed. "You desire her, eh?"

"But I don't even know her!" I shouted. I was blind with indignation.

"It doesn't matter. Often a man desires a woman he doesn't know, especially if she belongs to his friend."

Then, as if a theater curtain were suddenly drawn open, a dream came back to me that I had had at dawn: my friend's fiancée coming down an avenue, stepping slowly at first, running, and falling on me naked and out of breath; then taking my head in her hands and hugging it on her abundant breast.

If one could kiss her and twist her hand… under a dark bridge where the city lights and the river current would increase the suspense—because the sharper the tension, the better it is. And to lie in beached rowboats, with wide open eyes so as to see how she'd resist—whether she'd know how to surrender, because few women do. And above our heads would be the whole city, the bulk of the houses and the things that happen in them. Further on, river-boats at anchor would emit a homely smell of cooking food; dogs would be waiting with one eye open. Your friendship with the river is the first step towards knowing a city; and the second is to walk it through and through, to reach the utmost fatigue, so that if you were given a drop of water it would be a blessing.

The fiancée was born in a city of Asia. I didn't hear this from my friend but from my brother Phokion, who likes society gossip, spending, as he does, his days under the earth. Yet he seems to be used to dampness and the taste of iron, and all his movements are of one who belongs there: he passes from gallery to gallery, talks to a worker, orders another; he discusses things with engineers, leaning his head a bit to the side, as if the other person were telling him a secret. And he fastens his eyes upon the small ore-cart because the tools it carries are precious and expensive. He takes them in his hands, just as a violinist lifts his bow, and when laying them back in the tub he is careful how the tools touch each other. Often he does this work himself, not ashamed of being called a worker, as everybody knows he is not one. He alone knows how to make them fit together in a way that produces a special metallic harmony when the tub is moving. Though it is best when there is no sound at all, for this means a perfect arrangement and no danger of wear.

"Well, here comes Phokion," said Father, turning and glancing at him ironically as he entered the living room.

He looked at him in this manner often, although Phokion was the only one who obeyed him and followed him in the mines. Phokion was handsome, cold and indifferent. His hair was blond on the surface and brown underneath. He had a tall build.

"I don't think I'll be late," he said, looking at his watch and walking up and down with ease.

He was very well groomed and dressed rather formally. His pointed shoes somehow enhanced the nobleness of his face.

"Go bring the tool they sent us from the mine, so we can have a look at it," said Father, as if he hadn't noticed Phokion's clothes and his intention to leave. "They say it's damaged."

"Dorothea is expecting me," said Phokion firmly, "and it's time for me to go."

"You've all the time in the world," urged my father. "We are only going to have a quick look at it."

Phokion, suppressing a gesture of impatience, left the room and returned after a while holding the tool with perfunctory attention, without his usual tenderness. Then both of them bent over near the lamp and expressed their ideas about the repair needed. They changed a screw, but despite their careful handling, the tool slipped and Phokion's white silk shirt was soiled with thick machine grease. Phokion, unable to hide his anger, mumbled a curse. But it seems that this small mishap especially amused Father, and he started to recount other ludicrous incidents that occurred at solemn moments.

"Now I've lost the trend of my thoughts," continued Father, becoming very gay. He then spoke of a circus star, a monkey, who one day suddenly forgot her trick during the performance and was unable to remember it despite her master's prodding, his encouraging and cajoling words, and even his switch. She remained still, looking at the surrounding public with surprised and lost eyes, until they took her inside.

"Getting soiled is one of those tragi-comic things," I added, "as when one slips in the street."

"Yes, exactly, bravo, Alexander," cried my father. "From time to time you do say the right thing." He looked at me with pride and repeated, "As when one slips in the street."

Then I remembered the time I saw a woman's high heel catch against the curb; she tottered back and forth, finally losing her balance, and fell; and as I saw this I became dizzy till I thought it was I who fell, and wondered at my standing up. I wasn't able to help her up and the people in the street looked at me with a tinge of disdain, because although I was the one nearest, I had made no gesture to aid her.

Phokion in the meantime had gone to change his shirt; and perhaps fearing Father would make him look at the tool again, he left without saying goodnight.

"The rascal," said Father. He stirred in his easy-chair, made a movement to rise, and then changed his mind.

"Where's Aglaia?" he asked.

I remember how my sister Aglaia sobbed when she first became a woman. It broke your heart to look at her. Especially since she didn't know why she was crying. Now she sees things differently, for there is bound to come a moment when a girl becomes a woman. She was in the garden, in the light of the full moon, and lay flat on her belly under a willow tree, crying. She wept so much that her convulsed body shook against the earth, and her face, which she had buried in her hands, came free and also beat against the ground. I had to wipe from her face the mud of tears and earth.

"From this mud was man made," I told her.

But she pointed out that it was not possible, since tears didn't exist at that time. "It makes me feel good to cry now and then," she said. "It's as if my whole self were sinking and refreshing itself in water; nothing is drier than laughter."

This last observation was a lie of the moment for actually she liked to laugh and her laughter was crystalline.

These things happened at a time when we were tortured by the idea of sin—by the act itself; the thought of it had bothered us for a long time, and Aglaia's melancholy lasted half a year. She sat silent for hours with moist eyes and was careful to smooth down her skirt so that her legs wouldn't show; but at moments her look had an expression of bliss; and when it was cold outside and we lit the fire, her body and even her face became rounder. It was strange, for she was not heavy. Mother had nothing to say about this either. I don't know whether she even suspected it, but from time to time she stopped and looked at Aglaia as the girl passed from room to room. After all she had borne her and had all the right to look, even to ask questions. Though apparently she preferred to conceal everything, as the brooding hen her chickens: Grigori's story of the murder, this matter of Aglaia, Phokion's coldness, which she pretended not to notice, and my own laziness and all my other defects. I had an unlimited incapacity, Father said, and no sign of cleverness.

"It is the change that frightens me," Aglaia told me, "nothing else." Then I took her by the hand and led her inside where the whole family was gathered. "Aglaia is a woman," I said to them.

Aglaia lowered her eyes, or rather closed them, but soon opened them again and stared at everybody one by one. She stood beside me very straight, without stiffness.

Yet nobody seemed to understand and my words fell flat. Phokion even laughed foolishly, saying they knew very well that Aglaia was not a man and that I had said nothing new. We tried to be sincere; it was not our fault if they had not understood. So I took her by the hand again, and we went to the willow where I asked her to tell me the tale of the poor fisherman, which I never tired of hearing.

"Maybe it's all for the best," remarked Aglaia, "it might have caused trouble."

"Yes," I agreed. "Anyway, it doesn't really matter. Let everyone take care of himself. Grigori can look after his own affairs, Phokion and Father after theirs; as far as Mother goes—it's as if she knew already."

After the tale of the fisherman, we discussed Father's second family, revealing for the first time our curiosity and great impatience to know more about them.

"My dove," said Father, seeing Aglaia at the door, "I want you to prepare me a cup of camomile tea with your own little hands. I think I caught cold today down in the mines." He brought his hand to his throat and coughed. "Hot and sweet as only you know how. Just look at her," he said to me, glancing at Aglaia's delicate and harmonious body, "she is like a tiny Tanagra figurine."

When Aglaia came back with the camomile, he made her kneel beside him and lean her head on his knees; and while with one hand he lifted his cup to drink, with the other he stroked her hair.

"You know," he said after a while, and his voice had a bitter sweetness, "Alexander's friend is engaged."

Aglaia then lifted her head abruptly and looked at me with despair.

CHAPTER 3

All my energy went into ambition and voluptuous-
ness, and I can't say I regret it. I believed, for all that,
in an order of nature and felt great admiration for
things as different as ant hills and eagle nests. As for
sea gulls, the whole sea must be their nest, unless
they take shelter in rock hollows. The plashing of the
sea on the rocks and its regress to the infinite are
what I most admire and I thank Providence. When
by lamplight I hear the rumbling water, I go out and
walk for miles, sure that I shall meet my friend or the
woman of the ocean or even the one of the Saronic
gulf; and such things actually happen when I want
them very much and believe in them. Smoking alone
in a cafe is not a bad thing either. The others smoke
also, and your aloneness takes on another meaning;
there is an unspoken understanding, which exists as

well with the hurrying passersby if your glances happen to cross. You tell a story to another person and in the process of relating it, you elaborate on it, and so you always have new things to say and never are bored or feel you've come into the world in vain.

In the cafe I stretch my legs as far as they'll go, for they are long and fidgety and impede the nonchalance of my hands. But those who know me well, own that I fought in the war and took part in air-battles and dangerous missions. I'm not saying this to boast, but because it's the truth; and it answers Father who calls my generation worthless and who, in doing so, always stresses how he's never missed a day of work in his life and how many veins of metal he has found and that in general he doesn't know what rest means except for the fifteen days he took off because of the hot irons.

"Put two flatirons on the fire," Father had said to Mother one day.

He hadn't gotten up from bed and she turned and looked at him in surprise—not because of the irons, but because he spoke from bed. His habit was to jump up as soon as he opened his eyes.

"Your suit is already ironed," she said, "your shirts also."

"Put the irons on the fire I'm telling you, and bring them here."

Mother went inside, lit the fire and heated the flatirons. She went on with her housework completely mechanically, as if hypnotized. I often wondered whether she was conscious of her actions, and her whole attitude convinced me that one can spend a whole day coming and going, speaking and replying to questions, and think of nothing, not even of the things one is doing.

"Now burn the soles of my feet," Father commanded.

Mother took an iron, burned one of his soles, then took the other and burned the second; and when both were branded she realized what she had done and fainted.

Father stifled a groan for a moment, yet his face wasn't distorted; he was even able to say that now he would rest whether he cared to or not, since he would not be able to walk. The doctor had recommended at least fifteen days of repose. Fifteen days' rest in a whole lifetime. This is certainly different from my lying down without any reason and stretching out my legs in the cafe. Yet I fought in the war and rather fearlessly because I had adapted myself to that too. I was careful only about some details and superstitions concerning my life—as for example, I would not tell any of my comrades where my house was, because an address, they say, is necessary for a death notice.

After the battle, while we were still being called victors, our towns became infested with enemy soldiers. Of a day you saw them walking in the streets, you would come upon them at a turning of the road. Yet we had not spared anything for our defense. Their napes were thick and red and what is more, we had to serve them. As a prisoner of war my brother Grigori dug up corpses in the morning and in the afternoon peeled potatoes in a dimly lit kitchen. But road-building was heavier work than unearthing the dead. It was in this labor that his legs became stronger and he was prepared, so to speak, for the murder.

Yet it seems that famine and misery were widespread and the causes profound—it was a kind of plague or cataclysm sent by God. So after the cease-fire, hatred diminished and eventually in the waterfront cabaret, people did not bother to find out the next person's nationality. Everybody felt free to sing the songs of his own country, and, in communicating his nostalgia, the atmosphere of yearning became so dense, one scarcely knew which land to be nostalgic about or whether one felt closer to the sea, open plain or mountain.

For without having spoken about it, we knew this was not a war of besiegers and besieged. All of us, in fact, were within the walls and although fighting had stopped, the siege was not over. Our aim should have been to unite forces and raise the siege. Also we knew our sufferings were partly our own fault. Perhaps the situation was due to our own fear. It was as in a jungle where the strong animal is excited and attracted to devour the weak by the weaker animal's dread of being torn to pieces.

We had provoked calamity, but we could not have done otherwise. We had to taste from the tree of knowledge and even God himself could not have expected us to act otherwise.

To lust for what is not yours is a heightened pleasure; it is better to take than to be taken from. I'll never forget my relish when once I seized somebody else's wife. She, too, however, had a tendency towards sin and so my pleasure was diminished. It is one thing to make a ship in port lift anchor and sail to the open sea, and something else to give a new course of but a few degrees' deviation to a ship already at sea.

But the thin blond girl had not known the open main, and in the forest at twilight she seemed to look back for a long time. Her wide-open eyes were full and her vague smile had the bitterness, not of disappointment but of revelation, and the sadness that this moment of revelation had now passed. Then she started to cry exactly like my sister Aglaia. To change her reason for crying, I hugged her till I hurt her. Then she stopped altogether. And all her attention went to the bats and owls that had begun to fly about. The world of the

. so captivated her, she forgot she had seen
ɔpen sea for the first time.

"I'm afraid they'll get entangled in my hair," she
said, and from that moment on, this was her only
care. She put her hands quiveringly in her hair and
searched through it. And I was looking for a basic
law and meaning in the convulsion of her hands at
moments of intimacy, in the curve of her neck, in
the suspension of time caused at noon by the vertical sun over the beach, and in the sun-cut shapes
of salt where I tried to guess the face of my other
brother named *Alexander**—as Aglaia was trying to
guess the face of the other *Aglaia*. Both of us were
prompted by our great curiosity, a vague sympathy
and some fear.

Perhaps our thoughts also strayed to questions
of inheritance, although I don't really believe so.
Both Aglaia and I were idealists, but Grigori
laughed at us and was sometimes angry because
our ideals were not definite: it was high time for us
to acquire a set of real ideals, he said, we couldn't
wait till our hair was white. Our desolation was
immense and absolute and the rifts among us were
destined to become even wider since Grigori, I,
Phokion and Aglaia had each his own way of thinking. How then could I know the thoughts of my

---

* The italicized names refer to the illegitimate family.

other brothers and sister who must be more different since they were born of another mother.

Desolation everywhere. And only flashes of understanding—precious, perhaps, because of their rarity or intensity. They afforded us a palpable hope of something larger and more durable. We were all sad when somebody was seriously ill, we wept when someone else died and were glad about the births, which were not scarce in the family. We had cousins who were very fecund and we used to congratulate them with little packages tied up in pink ribbons for girls and blue for boys. Once, in the same morning after an aunt's funeral, we happened to utter our best wishes for a new birth. That day our family upheld the laws of balance and conservation of energy and it filled us with pride. This is what a large family can do—legitimate children to replace the dead, without even including those born out of wedlock.

My other brothers and sister were illegitimate. But when I first saw them, they didn't look it at all. The truth is I did not see their faces because I looked at them secretly from behind a garden fence. They were sitting round a table, eating, with their backs to the fence. I could only see their mother, a woman stronger than Mother, but with a colder face, perhaps more courageous, that is, visibly courageous. She was heavy, had wide hips, tremendous arms, and hands which became ten hands as they spread around the table; they were busy with cutting bread for one brother, serving food to another, wine to a third; they never stopped moving, as if anxious to hide her flat bosom. Her children had been reared on their nurse's milk.

"Lower your head," said my friend. "They may see us."

"Who do you suppose is *Alexander*?"

"Judging by the back, the one sitting in the middle. Your back is exactly the same."

"And what makes you think *Alexander's* back should look like mine and not like Phokion's?" I remarked. "He's the same relation to both of us."

"You're right, I hadn't thought of that," he replied. "I was taken in by the name."

We had to jump the wall, which was white, smooth, extremely tall. It circled behind an iron railing and thereby my *brothers'* and *sister's* house was doubly walled in. Pedestrians couldn't know this because they could see only the outer wall. Those who entered by the front gate did not notice anything odd: the outer door opened, they passed through and found the iron gate open too, and since the two doors were such a short distance apart, they seemed like one.

When my friend and I accomplished the feat of scaling the wall, we were impatient to see, and discouraged to find ourselves faced with a new barrier, impossible to climb; the bars ended in knife-sharp points which could have ripped into our stomachs. We had to look from behind the foliage, guessing rather than seeing. The one advantage was not being seen either. Finding ourselves between two barriers, the impassable iron bars in front, the wall behind frighteningly high and without a ledge to step onto, I must say our position was precarious. I found strength to climb the wall only because I was with my friend. Yet he didn't even give it a thought and whistled as he leaped over.

"Shut up, you fool," I said. "They'll hear us."

"Just don't make me laugh," he answered.

Then came my turn and I was fearful as ever that I would not make it and so lower myself in his eyes.

The house of my other *brothers* and *sister* was in the country outside of Athens—as ours was too, only ours was nearer the city. The mines were beyond the house and in order to reach them you had to pass by their door. My father had organized everything perfectly. He had the slyness and wisdom to build his two homes between the city and the mines so as to avoid a needless waste of energy and to be able to have a glimpse of his bastard children on going to and from work.

When they lit the north room, I could not tear myself away from that neighborhood. It had an irresistible attraction, as the sea gull island in the ocean which once I had wanted to reach by swimming, even at risk of my life, not knowing the futility of my efforts. When I got there the sea gulls flew into the air and all was deserted.

The light in the north room was so strong you could not see inside. The human forms lost their outlines, except for certain moments when, though a whole face could not be seen, you could make out a single detail thrown into focus: for example a nose or an eye. Perhaps my great eagerness blinded me, for my friend, who was foreign and indifferent, could see.

"Tell me," I asked, "tell me what's going on."

"*Aglaia's* come in."

"And?"

"She's looking in the mirror."

"Continue, don't stop."

"She's letting her hair down," he said.

"Go on, go on."

"I don't know, I can't see her any more. Wait, I'm beginning to make things out more clearly. Ah, there's *Alexander*. I didn't see him come in."

"Yes, yes, I see his right hand. He's holding a picture, two little children feeding ducks in a public garden. It is ridiculous to look at such a picture at his age. He's ridiculous, I'm telling you."

Then we hurried home because of the mist and

dampness. I think it was wintertime. We told Aglaia what we had seen.

"What do you think of *Alexander* holding up such a picture?" I asked her.

"Completely ridiculous," said Aglaia, lying on the sofa and closing her eyes in order to provoke my friend, although she was already married, a newly-wed.

"Let's have something to drink," suggested my friend.

"Yes," said Aglaia. "My husband will be late. He is at the mines. You know, although his position is somewhat less important than Phokion's, he doesn't drag tools around in a little ore-cart."

She stretched on the sofa and laughed—all women are the same at certain moments.

"Did you ever see Phokion towing his little ore-cart? And yet he's so dignified and perfect in society and well-lit rooms. It's unbelievable the way he pushes the tub down there in the dark, how tenderly he fondles the tools—each with a different feeling, now as if caressing a woman's hand, then her leg, then…"

"Aglaia, lower your skirt," I said.

She turned crimson. She rose, leaving her glass on the table, and sat down again, this time on the edge of the sofa with her legs placed neatly together.

"Dorothea's to blame for the way I'm acting tonight," she said. "It's all her fault. I never liked to drink. I hate her. I always have. I hated her from the very first moment. Forgive me please."

Then my friend got up, bowed to her and went to the piano.

"Tonight the scales are unimportant. I shall start directly with classical music."

CHAPTER 4

I felt wary of Dorothea when once I saw her sleeping, yet I didn't suspect she was the very same woman of the ocean. Then one day, I was taken aback as I opened the bathroom door by mistake and surprised her naked before the tub. She was going through the same movements as at the ocean and shaping the same imaginary forms, which now were ludicrous; her right leg and left hand were in the air and her face was bent over the steaming water to beautify her skin.

Though she had been Phokion's wife for fourteen months, it was only then I recognized her. I couldn't hold back a cry of surprise. She looked at me, naked and mute, and two waves of avowal and fear crossed her eyes.

"I've never been abroad," she said.

"And I suppose you have never tasted St. Peter's benedictine?"

"Are you crazy?" she said. "Phokion had warned me."

"Then be afraid of me," I whispered. And in order to humiliate her, I stared casually at all the details of her body, and especially at her elbows and knees, which were white, rough and scaly. I forced her to show her palms by making her turn over each hand.

For Dorothea, this was a capital offense. She was always careful to hide her palms. She never shook hands because, on contact, the scales and roughness seemed to increase and might even scratch someone. You would never expect this, seeing her general grace and beauty.

I knew her well, apart from unpredictable traits which every person keeps in reserve. Despite her hatred, she tried to reconquer me, perhaps only on the level of friendship, and before dinner she pretended to have forgotten the incident; she was gay and chatty, especially with me, and asked my opinion on the slightest matter. She knew how men are flattered by such things, how they like women to pretend ignorance and ask questions. She had a talent for this game, and both Father and Aglaia's husband fell into her trap. She would inquire about the mines: she said these things had interested her ever since she was a little girl. Then Father, Phokion and Aglaia's husband, all three people of the mines, competed in answering her questions. Dorothea recognized Father's preeminence, but said Phokion was also excellent, so that someday he might emulate my father; as for Aglaia's husband, he was nothing short of a phenomenon, considering he was a newcomer. During after-dinner coffee, we would break up into two groups: the three were talking shop with Dorothea; Grigori, Aglaia and I speaking of other things; and Mother in the middle, following both conversations.

Grigori rarely spoke to Phokion, and we all did our best to keep them from arguing. After the usual dinner-talk about food and weather, they inevitably ended up on the problems of our epoch. Phokion called Grigori a killer and a wrecker, and Grigori called Phokion a builder of rottenness and a bloodless murderer. Then, Dorothea, trying to put off the storm, would get up and dance, take one of them by the arm, laugh and nudge the other, laugh and clap her hands in the air and be altogether successful. She was a feast for the eyes, a living contrast to Aglaia who lost her equanimity easily, turned pale and whispered:

"It is unbearable to swim in the midst of two river currents."

Everybody turned and stared at her, just as if she had fallen among us from another planet.

"Sometime I would like to swim alone in the open

sea," she added, and as their astonishment increased, Aglaia was dismayed and became tongue-tied; she stumbled on the same syllable two or three times, and after a vain effort to express herself with gestures, she went to the window for privacy, lifted the tulle curtain and watched the thin rain. As the hour advanced, her gaze, sad at first, acquired such limpidity and calm, it seemed to obliterate obstacles, walls, and transcend all solid matter and distance. That is why then I told her about my travels, of how all the railway stations of the world are ash-gray at dawn with only a difference of density and hue, and about the shudder of trees before they lose their leaves—you walk through the park, it is raining, not a soul in it. And about the crossing of railway tracks and how you must be careful not to take the train that goes in the opposite direction. You arrive hoping you learn something, you leave with the bitterness of having learned nothing; hope is reborn during the journey and you are anxious to reach the next station, your hopes are soaring and the last five minutes are an agony of tension... and again the bitterness, a slight doubt at first and then the ripening into despair. And if you get over it, hope comes again that here at last you will learn—all with the regularity of flux and reflux. I remember how the water swelled at St. Peter and fishermen were preparing to set out as we heard the cry "Help, someone is drowning." A donkey came downhill loaded with two barrels of drinking water, and a crow and a sea gull crossed wings above the promontory rock that looked like an island. It was six o'clock when I thought that I was not at St. Peter and that the whole incident was a figment. I got up in wonder, and as I walked, found myself at the *Brave Sailor* inn. So again I was convinced that I, flesh and bone, was in St. Peter. I ordered a double benedictine...

"Stop, Alexander!" Aglaia said.

Aglaia caught me by the sleeve. As she gazed at the fine rain, she actually saw what I had said or left unsaid: Dorothea's silly self-admiration in front of the sea, the green sandals, the turn of the road where I started laughing and the night at the inn. Aglaia was so ready to receive messages that at moments she attained the power of reading thoughts and seeing into the distance. At other times she would not catch on to the simplest thing and many people thought she was not intelligent.

"Stop, Alexander, there will be a family scandal," she whispered.

Meanwhile, Dorothea, trying to smooth over my words, performed charming bits of nonsense and recounted jokes and small incidents which took on life only because of the simultaneous ripple of her hair, voice and breasts. Mother paid no attention to her and pricked up her ear in my direction for the simple reason that she had never traveled, had not even been away from her birthplace. The words "station," "lighthouse" or the name of a foreign city fascinated her. The differences of places and people are of course great, but she imagined them even more so, and wouldn't have been surprised had I told her that in the streets of a certain city, lions circulated freely or that people suddenly turned into rats and scurried into the sewers. She would become angry if I dared to draw parallels and say, for example, that children's voices after school are everywhere the same. At her insistence, I vividly described the moment a ship lifts anchor, the sound of its heavy chains, the behavior of people on the quay and passengers on the decks, and the high emotion when the anchor has been hoisted and the breeze becomes perceptible.

"Now, you must all hear about ship-cats," I said loudly, interrupting Dorothea. "Ship-cats lie on the canvas, waiting for a bird from a passing flock to tire and fall. But sooner or later some metal, used in building a ship, has a maddening effect upon them, and they commit suicide, jumping into the sea. Then the sailors are sad and lavish their love upon the dog; but in the next port, they are sure to acquire another cat, because boat-rats are a veritable scourge."

"Nobody asked you about ship-cats, damn it!" Father cried. "You always annoy us with such details of your travels, harping on animals and inanimate objects. You might at least say something about human customs. I'll never know why I handed out money all these years like a fool—for the boats and trains and then the hotels with a view, and you had to have a view. And may I ask, what are we supposed to be who live in darkness?"

He uttered this last sentence turning to Phokion and Aglaia's husband.

"You are the men of the mines," I said slowly and deliberately,

"So we can earn money for you to spend, eh?"

"That's it," I said.

As I waited for his anger to explode, for him to shout or strike me, I saw him raise his hand—of course, out of pride, I did not retreat an inch— he raised his hand and caressed my cheek.

"Yes, Alexander, for you I make my money, for all of you, and I always want you to choose hotels with a view."

He stretched out in his armchair, asked for another chair to lay his legs on, and retired into himself. He grew fatter every day, his voice became heavier; he needed more and more space, tore down low ceilings and never missed a chance to buy more land or undersoil.

"Our neighbor thinks he'll put one over on us, but he doesn't know me yet. I asked him for a map with a detailed outline of his property. I know what kind of ore it has, it's top quality. This is the last piece of land in our district belonging to someone else. I want it, though I don't want to be robbed either."

Then addressing Phokion and Aglaia's husband, he continued, "Listen, you two, have your wits about you, the *foreman* will be here any minute now with the plans. We must study them carefully. Why don't you stay too," he said to Mother, "so you can see the *foreman?* You haven't seen him since he was a baby and I ducked him into the baptismal basin. Do you remember what a splendid christening day that was, with everyone from the mines gathered in our front garden... 'I baptize the servant of God, *Phokion!'*"

"Here I am," said the *foreman Phokion*, kicking the door as he entered, his two arms loaded down with the plans.

He tried to greet everyone in the room with a slight nod, but he didn't succeed, unable to decide whom to begin with; he went to stand in front of one person, changed his mind and went to the next, and ended up by bowing to the empty space in between.

"One nod for all present would have been enough," said Father. "We don't have any time to lose."

Then the *foreman Phokion* tried to greet us with words, but he failed in that too, and so he made a general bow towards the window to avoid offending anybody.

"Unwrap the plans," said Father. "Untie the string first, you fool!" he thundered. The *foreman* had made all the movements of unwrapping the package, but to no avail, since he hadn't undone the string. "Look at him, he can't even undo a string… People would say you were completely helpless, if they didn't know you and if I didn't always declare that below ground you are my most competent worker, my right-hand man. It's the light that bothers him," Father said to us apologetically.

Meanwhile Phokion had come over to help. In front of Father he was responsible for the *foreman's* actions. He tried to get the plans, despite the *foreman's* unwillingness. As they stood facing each other, it became clear that the *foreman's* nose was much more pointed than Phokion's, almost exaggeratedly, and that his head was too big for his body. With a quick gesture, Phokion snatched the plans, and even more rapidly untied the string, so that the plans were unwrapped as if by themselves. He turned and looked at us proudly, letting out a cry like an acrobat after a dangerous feat; such was his enthusiasm that he threw out his arms and the plans rolled to the floor and scattered. The *foreman* with a bound collected them and brought them up to Father.

"Work begins," said Father. "End of the cock-fight."

"Now I remember the christening," Mother cried. "We killed twenty white roosters because an epidemic had struck the poultry, and we said it's better to eat them than to let them die."

But the three men and the *foreman Phokion* had already converged in a closed circle over the plans. Aglaia, while glancing through some musical scores, had dozed off to sleep. Her head leaned back with abandon; the lighted part of her face was gayer than the other half, and so was the illumined curve which began with her left shoulder and flowed down to the little finger of her left hand, continuing along the easychair. The chair itself resembled Aglaia and fit her like a glove. It changed shape and color according to her fatigue and the kind of weather.

"She is the only one worthy of relishing sleep," said Father, interrupting the study of the plans to everybody's surprise.

The *foreman Phokion* snatched this opportunity to leave. But Phokion, who was responsible, ran up and stopped him.

"Tonight is the union ball," said the *foreman*, "and I am in the orchestra."

Meantime Aglaia's husband had gotten up and with excessive tenderness placed a blanket over his wife.

"You relax your grip a moment, and off they go," Father murmured. "We barely sit down and there they are, scattered in the four corners of the room. Everyone back to his place," he called.

At that moment voices and music were heard. A group of musicians was passing by.

"These are the preliminaries for the party," said Grigori. "And don't look at me suspiciously, Phokion. I'm not hiding the fact that I took part in organizing the dance."

The *foreman* stood by the doorway and smiled.

"They are singing my song," he said proudly. "'The *foreman's* nose is sharp.'"

"Since you don't work in the mines, what right do you have meddling in the union dance?" Phokion asked Grigori.

"He is one of us," inserted the *foreman*, but again his attention was diverted and he smiled; voices could be clearly heard singing "The *foreman's* nose is sharp"; you could see the human river turning at the curb, a dark mass, with bright garish lights here and there, for many of the workers had forgotten to leave behind the lamps which hang on their caps as they descend into the depths of the mines, and it didn't seem strange to them to walk about with a lamp on their heads.

"Look at the day they choose for the dance," said Father, with a severe laugh. "It's snowing."

"It's good weather for the orchestra," said Grigori.

The human flood gradually darkened in the twilight, the black fences were becoming white (except for their very sharp points, which, as the snow could not settle on them, were set off like Chinese ideograms), and the dark-walled houses soon had white roofs.

"You can all go to the devil," said Father. "You can't settle down to serious work. And you," addressing the *foreman*, "I know what you need—to be kept overtime in the mines in order to study the plans; down there you don't dare think of anything else, you couldn't if you wanted to; I doubt whether you'd even remember the meaning of words like dance and music."

But the *foreman* was already dancing about and making noise. As he flexed his legs and looked at the ceiling, the disharmony between his head and body stood out, and his nose protruded shockingly. His trousers were baggy at the back. He was in constant danger of falling, because he kept stepping on his untied shoelaces.

"And now," said Father, turning to Phokion, "let the two of us at least prepare the article concerning our district for the encyclopaedia. I'll dictate: 'The inhabitants…'"

"In our parts the snow mixes with coal and becomes ash-colored," I intervened. "There are black footmarks everywhere. In the Alps it is supremely white with blue-green icicles on the peaks and you are impelled upwards to the next village or height. But still you know it is easy to come back. If the altitude is too much for you, you sleigh quickly down to a lower level."

"Son, let me bring you your woolen socks," said Mother, who loved Grigori most when it happened to be freezing cold. She remembered the time during the revolt when they put him in an outdoor prison, just a patch of land surrounded by barbed wire, and his feet were nearly frostbitten. She had feared he was lost to her forever, that they had shot him.

" 'The inhabitants are miners," continued Father, " 'a population of workers worthy of our respect. There is no daytime for the miner. He does not see the sun except on Sundays (and not then if it is raining). He descends to the innermost recesses of the earth, his body bent in two, often crawling. He disdains danger and accidents, which are none too rare. He is rather cheerful and believes in a God Protector of himself and his family. As for the metal, its utility is universally known: it is employed in the manufacture of household utensils and the highest quality war material of great destructiveness.' "

"I'm in a hurry to leave," said Grigori.

"I shall change them for you in a minute," said Mother, kneeling hurriedly in front of him with a clean pair of socks.

He had come back lean, dirty and bleeding after breaking away from the open-air prison; when she opened the door, she clasped hold of him. She had thought him lost. He pushed her aside rather roughly, but it didn't mean anything. At the moment, he could think of nothing else but food and sleep.

'Their way of escape had been simple. It was made possible because of a tent which cast a strip of shadow extending from the barbed-wire fence down to the sea.

"You must have eaten badly all these days, my boy," she had said to him. It was hard for her to say something appropriate.

"Oh no, they fed us on caviar."

Actually, it happened this way: the foreign jailers used to pass by in a truck and throw out cans of food—just a few, but enough for the prisoners to scramble over. Then the prisoners got organized: one common group was against the jailers, and several smaller ones fought each other during the tussle for the canned food. There were the workers' group, the consumptives' (they had arrested a whole sanatorium which was in revolt), the students', and besides these, there were a few lunatics who had taken part in the uprising from within their asylum. To make the strip of shadow, a tent had to be moved close to the barbed wire fence. Every day they edged it forward a few inches. The prisoners began to break away one by one, at four-minute intervals. When the searchlights were thrown on them and the first shots were heard, some came back pretending never to have moved from the camp, others surrendered midway and some slipped into the sea and remained motionless in the water, avoiding the least noise.

"When it's chilly, I want you to wear your woolen socks," said Mother. Carefully, she tied his shoelaces and tried to kiss his forehead. Grigori laughingly gave her two sonorous kisses on either cheek and Mother was radiant with joy.

"Father's godson the *foreman Phokion* is rather ridiculous," she whispered to us confidentially.

The voices grew louder and louder and the words became distinct because the instruments did not accompany the song itself. Drums sounded just before the singing began; and after it ended, the flutes came in. At the sound of the drums, the *foreman* jumped into the air kicking his legs right and left; with the refrain he stopped, and when the flutes started, he moved calmly and very slowly, imitating the movements of swimming, jumping over obstacles and flying. Grigori followed the scene with evident pleasure, apart from one or two moments when he looked out of the window, beyond the human crowd, with a kind of yearning. He came near Aglaia, collected two sheets of music that had fallen to the carpet, and placed them carefully on her knees. Then with sudden resolution, he took the *foreman* by the hand and hurried him outside.

"Do take into consideration," said Phokion to Father, seriously and with a touch of solemnity, "do consider that Grigori is corrupting the *foreman*."

"I'm not going to meddle in that," said Father. "The *foreman* is your responsibility."

"It's hard to fight against two—especially my brother Grigori and the *foreman Phokion*."

"When I asked you to be responsible for the actions of the *foreman*, you accepted," said Father. "And besides, I had warned you that the work of the mines is hard."

CHAPTER 5

"Tell me," said Grigori to the *foreman*, as he drew him out of the room, "is it true *Grigori's* written 'View onto the Sea' over the portal of his tavern?"

The *foreman* nodded in the affirmative.

"The son of a bitch," said Grigori.

"Son of a bitch," the *foreman* echoed, and he began to mutter incomprehensible words.

"What are you jabbering about?" Grigori asked.

"...that's why I insisted the dance take place out of doors. Our debt would only pile up."

Grigori caught him by the sleeve. It was twilight and snow was falling. The group with the musicians was passing.

"Wait a minute. You're hiding something from me."

"I said our debt would pile up."

"Speak," ordered Grigori.

"I should be running along," replied the *foreman*. "I am in the orchestra, the best drummer."

"All right, but that's beside the point."

"Yes, you should know about it. I do want you to know this." And leaning near Grigori's ear, he whispered, "Phokion can go straight to hell."

Grigori smiled. "Phokion deserves to be killed," he said. He seemed absent-minded.

"Yes," the *foreman* agreed, "Phokion ought to be killed." He in turn clutched Grigori's arm. "I am in the orchestra and I must be on my way," he continued.

"Speak," said Grigori.

"I'll never forget the things you taught us when you were a student, when you were still a boy, and…"

"That's beside the point," Grigori said. "Speak!"

"Well, it's this—the person who betrayed us during the revolt, who got us trapped, was my brother *Grigori*. The treason took place in the tavern."

"You don't mean it!"

Grigori halted abruptly and seized the *foreman* by the shoulders. He shook him strenuously and turned him around.

"I want to see your face," he said. "I want to see whether you're telling the truth. I know you hate him as I hate him. As we both hate Phokion."

"Phokion should be killed," the *foreman* murmured. "And when my sister *Aglaia* gives birth, I won't let him see the baby."

"In *Grigori's* tavern we did such excellent work," Grigori said. "He was our confidant. How is it possible?"

"He plays a double game," replied the *foreman*, "and not only that, but even now he's up to something new. He is dangerous."

"I must see your face. I must know if this is true."

He dug his fingers into the *foreman's* shoulders and shook him violently.

"Leave me alone, Grigori, leave me alone I'm telling you. We have proof of it. Go to 130 Aristides Street, and you'll learn everything, even what's going on today, there are proofs, and here's my face."

From his pocket he brought out a miner's flashlight, and held it under his chin to light up his whole face, and then moved it around his face, stopping now in the right eye, now in the left.

"Stop that," cried Grigori. "It's unbearable."

Grigori struck the flashlight, which fell into the snow. He started to run.

"You're missing the union ball," the *foreman* yelled after him. "Though you would have only been a spectator. 130 Aristides Street! 130 Aristides Street!"

CHAPTER 6

Midway through the ball, at the height of the party, a rider came to tell the *foreman* that his sister *Aglaia* was in labor. The *foreman*, not understanding at first, smiled and went on playing his flute. Yet the *rider* insisted. There was no time to spare, he said. This was the postwar period when there were many childbirths and the clinics were so full that often three or four women were giving birth at the same moment in the operating room. All about the room were crying children and screaming women; the doctor moved from one to another; the women uttered wild shrieks and the little ones bleated tenderly like kids, and some of them miaowed; a dozen or fourteen babies weeping in the operating room during childbirth, and naturally they were the only fitting company, the only relief for the women in labor during the moments of pain and tearing, of bulging eyes and flooding sweat and irrepressible screaming.

"We must arrange for a bed," said the *rider*. "There are many women due to give birth tonight."

Then some couples came near and complained that the music had stopped. As the dance was taking place in the open air, care had been taken to trample down and smooth out the snow, and people had dressed as warmly as possible. Only the musicians were sheltered under a pavilion and were entitled to two glasses of wine instead of one, and well-filled at that. Ever since a fire set by the local shepherds, the pines were scrawny and sparse, red rather than green.

"What would you like me to play for you?" asked the *foreman*.

But he must have suddenly remembered what the *rider* had said to him, for he flung his flute into the snow and leaped up behind on the horse.

"Give 'er the whip, *Alexander*," he said.

Now the orchestra was inadequate. This prompted the men to go after the women sooner than might have been expected, completely abandoning themselves to life—and not even their slyness could save them from its impact, from the call of the blood which possessed them as they merely fondled a woman's bosom.

The musicians got down from the stands and

mixed with the dancing couples; people who had never played a musical instrument were trying out the flute and drum for the first time. The musicians danced, leaving their sheltered platform to couples and their now unavoidable embraces. The birthrate was certainly not going down because of these chance meetings. There was, in fact, a steady increase since the war, and every day the world was filled with new babies.

But many people had also died in battle, in air raids at home and at the front. Whole villages had disappeared as if sucked in by a volcano, swallowed intact at a given moment, with their central square, cafe, church and barber shop, leaving only two big stones to mark their place on the map. And of course there was dying from starvation, long deaths, because you never knew when they began; people were dying for days, months, perhaps a year, begging for a crumb or for the spirit to leave the body. Often they happened to breathe their last at the corner of a main street in the heart of the city where they sat doubled over to postpone the final agony, which came, however, always a little too soon, while the policeman at his post directed non-existent cars to give an impression of busy traffic. The one kind of death which seldom occurred was suicide because of love. Women were not difficult. If you wished to die, you could choose a more heroic way out, such as a submarine trip into enemy waters or a parachute leap behind enemy lines.

"And why do they give us only one drink?" cried someone.

Then voices were heard from all over:

"We want wine, we want wine."

From this moment, the men turned their attention to getting drinks. The women were somewhat stunned by their sudden abandonment; some buttoned up their blouses and smoothed down their tightly curled hair, which, in relation to rather short legs, made their heads seem enormous and awkward; but after the first surprise, they also clamored:

"We want wine…"

"You can't have a party on one drink," yelled one of the younger men, "the union should've taken care of it."

"Who's speaking against the union?"

"Yeah, they should've seen to it," cried another.

"Who's talking against the union?"

"It's badly organized," cried the younger men.

Before one knew it, they had taken sides. But at the instant they were about to clash, the women thrust themselves between the two groups, whining it would be a shame to spoil the ball which was such a rare event, and why not go to *Grigori's* tavern where there were barrels of wine and where they could sing and dance.

"Those sluts sometimes have the right idea," said a middle-aged man, laughing uproariously. Then he became more serious and gave the signal.

"Come on, let's go to *Grigori's*."

The musicians led the way in order to set the pace. It had become much colder, their teeth were rattling and the women's legs were chilled to the bone.

Some people tried to tear down the stands, but their hands were numb, as if their fingernails were falling off. They took down one or two planks and then went on. Everyone made an effort to give a gay tone to the march. But it was not easy. They were beginning to feel the cold too acutely. They started a song, it faded away; then another more daring verse that met with the same fate. The women tried to laugh as if someone were tickling them, but they didn't carry it off. They all straggled along as fast as they could, and their only thought was of the warmth of *Grigori's* tavern—and perhaps of their desire to return home, though no one would ever say so. The dance had begun and it had to go on to the end. In any case, at *Grigori's* the temperature would be milder and there would be barrels of wine and the *owner* offered credit. They lit their lamps again and hung them from their caps, although it was full moon and the way was familiar. Whenever the musicians remembered, they sounded the drums; the last ones in the group were dragging the dismantled planks over the snow. Nobody said a word.

Grigori's tavern lay between the mines and the farm-lands. It was the borderline. Thus its clientele was mixed and there was a variety of talk: the farmer spent his day differently from the miner, and the weather meant something else to each one. Those who planted wheat prayed for rain during certain months; the vineyard owners wished it to come at other times. Small landowners and tenant farmers and workers of every description met there. At vintage time, after sundown, it was so full, if one dropped a pin it wouldn't hit the floor. On St. Demetrius' day the new wines were opened and winter followed soon after. Beyond the fields was the sea. You could not make it out, however, except on very limpid days. Nevertheless, when the sea wind blew, you thought of storms, your hair stuck together, and bread and your skin were scented with salt.

The tavern was far from the houses, but not off the main road; it was situated at a curving of the highway which ran from Athens to the sea and on to the ancient temple at Sounion. Cars stopped for refreshments or gasoline—everybody said it was the great stroke of genius in *Grigori's* life to have installed a gasoline pump by the tavern and to have learned to fill tires and do small repairs.

"Good Christ, where did all the blood come from?" said the first musician as he went in. He lifted his legs, and looked at the soles of each shoe. "Damn it, right in front of the door."

"Another accident," said *Grigori*.

"Be careful not to step in the blood," said the first musician to the others. "There was an accident."

"Wine," said the men.

"What happened? Let's hear about it," the women called.

"Never mind the women. We've come for wine. This is the night of the union ball."

"I know," said *Grigori*. "My brother, the *foreman*, told me about it. I also knew you wouldn't be able to hold out for long in the open air on just a drop of wine. I've taken care of everything. There are snacks and plenty of records, the latest hits."

The women went wild with enthusiasm. In an effort to outdo one another, each sang her own song.

"The wretches, they're only good for the bed," cried someone, and everybody laughed. There was already plenty of wine, and it was warm.

Grigori moved back and forth filling the pitchers. He limped a bit on his left leg. He also had been in an accident on the curve. The cars should slow down at that point, and there was always talk about putting up a sign as a warning, but that was the State's affair. Besides, they were accustomed to accidents. *Grigori* could recount all the accidents that had occurred ever since he owned the tavern, and how each time he had had a presentiment.

"I'm going to see if there's any blood on the highway," said one of the women.

She wanted to get up, but everybody held her down. Why upset the party?

"You better have a drink."

They forced her to gulp two glasses in a row. She laughed and insisted on going outside.

"I'm going to see if there're any blood stains on the road."

"Drink."

And they filled her glass. It was just what she wanted. She was laughing.

Suddenly *Grigori* said, "We have killed God, we have lost our face."

Everybody understood. He was high. Before getting drunk, he always said these words, seriously and staccato, as if giving an order. Gradually, with the help of wine, he incorporated them into songs; then they became the only words and changed tune according to his mood.

"The sky is cloudy, the sky is cloudy," a woman sang in a strident voice.

The phonograph was playing "Open your door, I can't go on."

"The sky is cloudy, rain is falling," continued *Grigori*. "We killed God, we have lost our face."

"He's all lit up," exclaimed someone. "Here's to you, *Grigori*."

"And why shouldn't God be killed?" put in somebody else. "Why should *we* be killed?"

"I suppose you're killing yourself working, loafer."

"We're killing each other at the border," said a third.

A silence fell. The record ended and the needle scratched in the empty groove.

"Wait a minute," cried another. "Stop swearing and saying that God should be killed, or I'll break your neck."

"Well, look then, we've had wars and now a civil war. The only thing missing was a sea monster to come and devour us all. And now the good Lord sends us a sea monster. You read about it in the papers, didn't you? Why shouldn't He be killed then? What could that little child have done to be eaten up in two bites by a shark? What was the shark doing in our waters, anyway? As for what's going on at the border…"

"Don't begin again or I'll break your head."

He got up, ready to fight. Again the women intervened.

"Let's dance," they proposed. They were excited.

"And we lost our face," *Grigori* sang in a low voice, but his gestures denoted a certain restlessness. Now and then he went to look out of the door. He was waiting for word from his sister *Aglaia*. It would be her first child. It was hard being a widow in the first year of marriage. The young director Phokion had assigned her husband to one of the most dangerous tasks in the mine. A boulder had broken loose and crushed him. Phokion seems to have felt his responsibility; he helped her more than was considered normal. He even visited her. After all, she was also his father's godchild and had every right to be protected.

"I'll break your head!"

This time the man was too quick for them. The blow flew and landed square on the head of the other, who tottered and fell back against the table. There was havoc and broken glass; his nose began to bleed. Wine and blood ran from the edges and cracks of the table. The women got up, crying: "He was wrong. Why did he hit him? He wasn't swearing any longer."

"But he was laughing," said the attacker.

"Doesn't one have the right to laugh?"

"Yes, but his laugh was like cursing. It was insolent."

"Oh what the hell," said *Grigori*, gathering up the broken glasses. "This is the union ball."

But he was thinking of *Aglaia*. Perhaps she was giving birth that very moment; a terrible shout and the child would come from her insides.

"You're going to pay for that," cried the man who was hit, as soon as he came to. He was ready to strike back.

Everybody rushed between them. It was stupid to ruin the party. They held them apart.

"Wine!" they called. "Wine."

The phonograph started again: "Open your door, I can't go on."

"Take your hand away, you're tickling me," a woman giggled.

Her neck was trembling, her breast heaved up and down. The women were in hysterics of laughter. The men turned to kissing them on the nape to stop it. But the laughter increased. They pinched their arms. To no avail. Somebody tried to tell a story of a tamed gull who lived on land, who ate cottage cheese and slept in a chicken coop. They called him Marco and he answered to his name. The storyteller, however, could not be heard. The women were frenzied and you could only quiet them by force, by hurting them. The world was filling up with babies. And this despite civil war and stories of children in the country and at the border who had become neurasthenic and had nightmares. In the hospitals, those who had the most terrifying nightmares were separated from those who simply had nightmares, so that during the night they would not all cry at the same time and drive each other mad. But there were also children who, having grown up amid bombs and whistling of artillery shells, did not recoil an inch on hearing a round of shots and strolled about or played marbles in the square at the moment a village was changing master. They had never known a time of peace: before it was the years of world war, and now the civil strife.

"We have killed God, we have lost our face!"

Now *Grigori* was singing loudly, with rage. It seemed that his soul would leave him. He opened the door and looked outside.

"Did your brother *Alexander* pass by here?" I asked.

"Who are you?" *Grigori* asked me.

"Tell me, tell me whether *Alexander* has been here."

"Yes, he came to pick up my brother *Phokion* because *Aglaia* is about to give birth. But who are you?"

"Which way did he go?" I said.

"I don't know. But who in the devil…? Oh, I get it," *Grigori* said after a pause. "You must be Alexander, the son of my godfather who's master of the region. Haven't you had enough? Do you still insist on seeing him, even though he avoids you?"

There was a clattering of horse hoofs.

"Our sister *Aglaia* has given birth," said the other *Alexander*, as he came to a halt. "She's doing well. It's a fat boy. No, no, I don't have time to come in. Not even for a glass of wine. Goodbye."

"*Alexander!*" I shouted. "*Alexander*, stop!"

He had already disappeared.

"*Aglaia* has had a son," announced *Grigori*, going back inside.

They were all asleep, some on the floor, in heaps, others flat on the table. They were snoring.

"Hey, my *sister's* had a child, do you hear?"

No reply. Their faces were indifferent and far away.

"Who can I tell it to?" *Grigori* muttered. He went to shake them, one by one. "My *sister's* had a baby, do you hear? That's why I treated you and wouldn't even charge for the glasses. My *sister's* had a fat boy. *Alexander's* just come to tell me. He came on horseback and the other fellow cried 'stop' but of course he didn't. What a pack of asses! Just when I want to speak, no one listens. Look at this, I kick them and they don't move. Might as well kick a rock. All right, I'll make all of you pay—for every broken glass. A fat boy, do you understand? He told him to stop, but he didn't stop. Did you get that? Do you hear that?"

He went to the door and opened it.

"We have killed God, we have lost our face. You brutes, I'll make you pay for those glasses!"

CHAPTER 7

"Nice day to get drowned in the ocean," Dorothea had told me earlier in the evening with a touch of hidden meaning in her voice. It was just at the time the workers' dance was beginning and Grigori was leading away the *foreman*. Then, after teasing Phokion, who had complained to Father about Grigori spoiling the *foreman*, she added, "I miss benedictine and going abroad."

I took her hand. She thought I was yielding to her.

"So, you have been abroad," I said summarily.

I looked insistently at the rough palms of her hands.

"I miss benedictine," she repeated, as if she were giving herself to me.

"Your body is beautiful," I murmured, "but your palms are dry."

She was angry.

"And you have a senseless way of admiring yourself in front of the sea."

"Phokion," she cried, "I'm going up to my room." And turning to Aglaia, who had begun to read a musical score, "This isn't a house, it's a bedlam," she said. "What is the *foreman* doing here anyway, while we're drinking our coffee? And why should Father have given him Phokion's name?"

"As a matter of fact, it's Phokion who got the *foreman's* name," Aglaia replied. "The *foreman* is two months older."

"Either way, it's the same. What a queer mania to give your godchildren the names of your own children. Phokion, I'm going to my room."

Then turning to me, she said, "I just bought the record *Les enfants qui s'aiment* and I'm going to try it out. Would you care to hear it?"

Of course it would not have cost me anything to hear the record and I certainly didn't have any qualms about being alone with my brother's wife. But I was thinking of the ball and whom I might meet. To go upstairs, hear the record just once and then leave was not at all plausible. For once in her room, the atmosphere of warmth, music and drink crept over you, and you couldn't leave. I wouldn't say these attractions were irresistible, but as they were pleasant and restful to the point of numbing you, the nightly walks and the searching became absurd and you asked yourself why struggle when there are armchairs.

"Some other evening," I said.

Then she was really angry and slammed the door behind her.

I imagined her undulating body as she went up the stairs. She rang the bell, ordered a drink, and from her room we could hear *Les enfants qui s'aiment*. The proprietress of the inn cooked excellent sauces, but she used too much salt and pepper, and that night we hardly stopped drinking water. It was almost comical—the amount of water we got down. All the time we were putting the light on and off in order to drink. She rang again for more wood for the fire. It was really at an ocean beach, I don't have the slightest doubt, and I wonder how I could have been so confused at one time. The two places were quite dissimilar—both in nature and climate. She rang the bell once again. She didn't like the brand of the liqueur that was brought to her. She preferred the kind she had the Saturday before, yes, the one with the red label.

"Why don't you go and listen to the record?" Phokion asked me suddenly.

He showed a certain nervousness after receiving a telephone call some time before. He kept changing seats and his cigarette lighter, normally in perfect order, wouldn't light. At table, he had begun a conversation with Mother, and this was indeed rare; he even asked her whether she had suffered much when she gave birth to him.

"What's the matter, Phokion?" I said.

"I'm asking you why you don't go and listen to the record. Besides, it's warmer upstairs."

I understood that if I were to go he would consider it a favor, so it would have been silly for me to have any moral compunctions. In fact, I regretted my refusal as I imagined Dorothea going up the stairs. After the record I would be able to stretch my legs as far as I liked, and put them under Dorothea's low little table in front of the fireplace. "You are a wicked child," she would say, and everything would be easy, pleasant and warm.

Les enfants qui s'aiment—she ought to have played it more slowly; its rhythm was meant to be slow-time. I was ready to go tell her. I stood up. But a dog barked.

"No, Phokion," I said, "I won't go up to Dorothea's right now. I'm going out to get some air."

It must be time for the union ball to begin, I thought. And afterwards... the long watch, the lurking around outside *Grigori's* tavern—with the patience of the hunter, plunged in the marsh up to his knees, waiting for the passing of flocks.

Phokion was forced to go upstairs. There was one floor for both couples, Aglaia and her husband,

Phokion and his wife. They shared a sitting-room and a radio. But the phonograph was Dorothea's. She had it next to her bed, with her large collection of records.

"Take that off, will you? It makes me nervous," said Phokion as he came in.

"It amuses me," said Dorothea.

"It's the fifth time in a row you've put on the same thing."

" I bought it today, that's why. If it bores you, go to your own room."

Ever since the fourth month of their marriage, they had separate rooms. Dorothea liked to play solitaire in the evenings and kept the light on very late into the night—sometimes until dawn if she had insomnia. Phokion usually came back from the mines dead tired and wanted to sleep.

"You and your sister. She's also been nervous, and pretends to have heartburn. Actually, all her agitation is because she hates me."

"Aglaia is different," said Phokion. "She likes being alone and abhors discussions."

"Is that why she hardly stops talking when we have guests? Why her eyes shine and she never sits out a dance?"

"Yes, it's true," said Phokion. "She is either silent or very talkative."

"And the slightest draught gives her a cold, yet she bathes in the sea all through the winter; she hardly grasps what you tell her, yet she happens to guess your thoughts. Believe me, she's the craziest one of the family, and Alexander follows close behind. She said she couldn't breathe, and her heart was going to break."

"So she's full of anxiety too?"

"What do you mean?"

"Wasn't that the telephone?"

"Not to mention the things the two of them talk about. Before the *foreman* came in, Alexander gave her a lecture about his travels. But he is a liar. You mustn't believe all he says. St. Peter doesn't produce benedictine; it is made in the next village, which is almost a town. That's why Aglaia stopped him—and also to show him an excerpt from a book she was reading, something demoniacal, about alchemists who sought disharmony in matter itself and spoke about cold fire and black sun, and suddenly Alexander bent towards her and whispered: 'Father makes practical experiments at our expense, without caring about our agony,' and then…"

"Yes," said Phokion, "Aglaia won't sleep tonight. Her difficulty in breathing was real, her heart is truly going to break. But didn't that sound to you like the telephone ringing?"

"Give me the cards to play solitaire… there, in the night-table drawer, on the right."

"I must be going," said Phokion. "It's snowing,

but in here it's so hot, I'm sure to fall asleep. I mustn't let myself doze off. There's some business at the mines. What's the matter? There's nothing so odd about a late appointment. At any rate, this is a matter concerning the mines, which I can't explain, and it would bore you if I did."

"Stay, Phokion, I won't play solitaire. We shall play cards together."

"No, they're expecting me," said Phokion. "You'll never have a child."

"Give me the cards!" she shouted.

Phokion had already left.

Then Dorothea began to think about Aglaia's husband, who was moderate in his politics—one might call him a liberal, more or less—and a very handsome man. He loved Aglaia with insistence, he covered her when she fell asleep in the armchair, and then turned around to look at Dorothea, as if to say "Ask me about the mines." She thought of smashing the record, because she was tired of it, and also to make some noise. Aglaia's husband was sensitive to sound…

"What's the matter, Dorothea? Do you need anything?" He was already knocking discreetly on her door.

"Yes, do help me pick up these broken pieces. These last days, things just slip from my hands."

He stooped down in front of her.

"Don't go yet, let's have a drink."

She shuffled the cards.

"What about a few games? Here, in front of the fire."

"Aglaia has heartburn, and perhaps I should… yet it is very pleasant here. Give me another glass."

"The union ball has thrown the family into confusion," said Dorothea laughing. "Don't you think so? All of them looked so changed tonight, except us two. In fact, what are we doing in the middle of it all?" She laughed again. "Every time Grigori and Phokion quarrel, you soothe them with well-chosen words and a convincing voice, and I with dancing. Why should they insist on going out into the snow when here we have good central heating?"

"And deep easy-chairs," added Aglaia's husband.

"It is Alexander who gives the signal for this kind of craziness. And he incites Aglaia too. They read strange books and speak of black suns."

"Listen, Dorothea, I didn't want to tell this to anybody, but when Aglaia had difficulty in breathing, she was saying, 'Help *Aglaia*,' and when I asked what was the matter with her, she told me, 'There is nothing the matter with me. Help *Aglaia*.'"

"What do you say about playing a hand?"

"Right. Give me the cards so I can deal."

How hard it is to breathe and live, thought Aglaia, yet it is beautiful to walk about in the morning and swim. He didn't understand her agony over the growing pains of the other *Aglaia*. He was playing cards with Dorothea when *Aglaia* was to give birth at any moment. Phokion had already received the telephone call. At that very moment she may have been torn with pain, bending the iron bars of the bed, not knowing where on the mattress to put her belly and waist that were opening up; she may be tossing about not knowing where to put hands and legs, everything being in the way, and her head, if at least she could crush her head against the wall and cease to know she was suffering, and let the convulsion of pain, that looks like laughter, remain petrified on her face. He didn't understand, yet he covered her with excessive tenderness. What did it matter if he turned to look at Dorothea? After all, Dorothea was interested in the mines, and she asked questions and then listened attentively, unlike herself who was often absent-minded, and surely it's futile to talk to an absent-minded person. Dorothea said the mines were her passion, and said it laughingly so as to emphasize the simultaneous ripples of hair, voice and breasts—yet the sadness of her eyes remained—and she was able to hide the roughness of her skin and her dry palms. It was Aglaia's own fault, Dorothea would say, if she never learned how to play cards, she couldn't tell a King from a Jack. Still, Aglaia thought, Alexander's friend, after the final note of the last piece of music, turned and looked at her. She knew it, and her eyes were ready for that second, which afterwards she brought back to mind systematically and with a self-lacerating insistence, once, twice, three times, yet it dimmed, and she was left with but the agonizing will to preserve it from being completely dimmed and lost; we must keep the second, we must imprison it, build a tall wall around it with high iron bars to prevent it from going away, even at the risk of being swallowed up by the second as it sprawls and occupies the whole of space.

Aglaia's bed must be too narrow, since no amount of space is big enough when one is giving birth, not even the earth itself. By now the earth must be filled with her body and the last shriek of childbirth, there can be no space left for houses, for rivers, nor for trains passing into tunnels, space is too narrow, *Aglaia* is suffering, the earth is narrow and even if the rivers and houses were to disappear, the earth is narrow and she is in pain.

"Ace of hearts."

Dorothea's laughter was heard.

"That's my game," Dorothea was saying. Here she did not have to fear the ocean, or the vacuum in the atmosphere which her hands had felt that other time. Here she could touch the glasses and shuffle the cards: she shuffled them with astonishing speed.

"Are you always so nervous?" Aglaia's husband asked.

He watched her move around the table.

"The cards are slipping through your hands. Don't worry. I shan't pick them up for you. I know you let them fall so you can bend down to the carpet. You keep the glasses and the drink in different places, in order to find a pretext to move about."

"You're clever," replied Dorothea. She stopped laughing, and the sadness in her eyes became more marked.

"Did you have any doubts about it?"

"Do you know, Phokion is beginning to fear you."

"For what reason?" he said, leaning abruptly over the table.

He was almost touching her. She too bent imperceptibly forward, and drew back just as quickly. She was laughing.

"No, not because of me," she smiled. "No, he is afraid of you because of the mines. He fears you may take his position."

"He is afraid of the *foreman* too. I am also, for that matter."

"Do you mean to say you're afraid of that ridiculous creature who can't pronounce a single word properly, who only knows how to sing 'The *foreman's* nose is sharp'?"

"In the mines he is strong. He dominates us," Aglaia's husband said.

"Not the old man though. All of you fear the old man, and the *foreman* fears him most of all. He is the only man around here," she said, and began to move around the table.

"Dorothea, stop that, you make me giddy."

"How dare you? I do what I please, and I'm going to go round and round as much as I want, and I'll scatter the cards on the floor just in order to pick them up afterwards. There!"

She dropped the cards and stamped on them crying.

"Hysterical," murmured Aglaia's husband, and then he said more loudly:

"Dorothea, your legs are beautiful, especially the shape of your thighs. I would like to have a hundred packs of cards to scatter, only to see you stamp on them."

CHAPTER 8

"Take this pill, Aglaia, and get some sleep. That way you won't feel a thing," her husband told her, after coming back from the first round of cards with Dorothea.

"Who's ahead?" Aglaia asked him.

"I, of course. She only knows how to shuffle the pack."

"I detest her," said Aglaia.

"I adore you," her husband said. He helped her rest her head on the pillow and covered her up.

"*Aglaia's* bed must be narrow," she said.

For no space is sufficient, not even the earth it-self, she thought.

"With this pill, everything will be all right. Now rest."

By now the earth must be filled with her body and the last shriek of childbirth.

"Do swallow the pill," her husband insisted.

There could be no place left for houses, rivers or underground trains.

"These are the best pills," he repeated.

"Help *Aglaia*," she cried, and then, grabbing the packet of pills, she threw it out of the window.

"Don't you see that I want to feel, I want to see everything, feel everything. And not to confuse houses with trees. I am in pain as *Aglaia* is, and perhaps I shall know her tonight. I mustn't fall asleep and fade away. It's terrible that everything drifts away, drifts away unperceived, we don't care enough to say this is a house, here is a tree, nor do we distinguish the flavor of sugar from salt, and we wander from room to room like draughts of wind."

"You are jealous of Dorothea. I assure you…"

Yet, Aglaia thought, if you see a half-house you can't very well call it a house. For there are houses rent in two with the precision of a cut watermelon, in one place because of the Civil War, in another because of the bombardments. And there are slices of houses, one wall standing, leaning painfully on an adjacent building. Today she saw the fiancée in the street, quite by chance, and her blond hair and full figure were silhouetted against a house cut away into vertical segments. You could see the interior and the half-rooms, the pipes and pegs on the wall and a gold frame without a picture. The furniture, although scorched, had been stolen, and from time to time people came to rip away planks from the flooring. Without the roof, the floor was of no use, exposed, as it was, to the full impact of wind and rain.

"Yes, I know," Aglaia said, "it's that Dorothea is also interested in the mines."

She took his hand and caressed it.

"Too bad," she said.

Yet she didn't have time to call the fiancée. Perhaps she lacked the boldness. She ran after her, almost touched her shoulder, and noticed how her neck and hair were carefree. Then stopping, she saw her disappear in the crowd. But she should have called her and talked to her. She should have talked about anything, about the half-houses, for example, or about the water pail. It hadn't been stolen and was hanging precariously between the second and third floor. The fiancée would have said yes— at just this moment the sailors toss a pail into the sea in order to wash the deck. The deck has to be sparkling clean and the ship must smell of cleanliness. An airplane has a special odor, Alexander had told her, which does not resemble that of a ship or a car, which pilots adore and prefer to women's perfumes. God, she should have called to her and spoken. This was the fifth time she had missed her chance, but she would certainly call to her when she saw her again. For she saw the fiancée quite often: each time she wandered at random to meet Alexander's friend. Instead of him, she met the fiancée. She turned into a street, the fiancée, went down another, again the fiancée, into a cafe, the fiancée, in the theater, the morning, the afternoon, the fiancée, blond and carefree. And Alexander's friend would touch the fiancée and kiss her. Suddenly in the night, he would seize her by the waist, and hug her and hug her... My God, why didn't she stop her and tell her, please, do not ever see Alexander's friend again. It wouldn't be difficult. She would begin with "Please" or "I beg of you" or "I implore you", the fiancée would reply "but of course" or "with pleasure" and "if I ever encounter him, I'll cross to the other side of the street."

"I assure you there is nothing between Dorothea and me. It is simply that she has insomnia and is afraid of being alone."

"I know that tonight my hatred for Dorothea will be lessened. Why should sadness never leave her eyes and why does she go through the same movements before the bathtub as at the ocean, the senseless figures in the void, never finding a point of support? She gets up at eleven-thirty and yet, with all her mad running around, why does her day never seem to end?"

Dorothea had made her suffer very much by her manner of laughing and the way she took Aglaia's husband by the hand just when he wanted to cover her; by the way she uttered a cry just at the moment he wanted to look at Aglaia in silence.

"We grow a little further apart every day," she said. "And I begin to wait again for the postman as I used to do in the Alps."

"Listen," her husband said, "I'll play one more hand. Dorothea's afraid to stay alone."

"I can't bear half-houses," Aglaia stated.

"She told me she has nightmares even when she's not sleeping. Phokion's gone out. What has happened to all of them tonight? The bedrooms are empty. They speak about a mission. What kind of mission is this that makes them all want to kill each other?"

"Phokion wants to come face to face with the *foreman*," Aglaia began. "The mines are no longer big enough for the two of them. Whoever moves more quickly will destroy the other. Grigori wants to show that he believes in fire. And Alexander runs after the other *Alexander*, and becomes embittered and walks miles when he might have known him without lifting a finger. And I suffer the pain of the other *Aglaia*. I am *Aglaia*. I don't want to think of anyone else: neither the postman, nor the fiancée whom I didn't have the courage to stop, nor of Dorothea's eyes. Let Alexander's friend hug the fiancée as much as he likes. He's gone far enough in filling my thoughts and taking me away from *Aglaia*. Tonight I want to think only of *Aglaia*, and now I see the whole thread from the time I was born and began to play. What lucidity, good Lord, a transparency in the landscapes. If I could, if I could only keep this lucidity… And as for our drifting apart, which began when Dorothea married Phokion, and you watched her go up the staircase, this drifting apart filled me with horror and agony, my breast swelled, swelled, and I wondered how to contain myself, what place would hold me, I ached and the walls stepped toward me, advancing a few steps each day, until the roof came loose and fell and crashed, and the pressure was so great that I was freed. I hurled the broken panes through the window, yes, I see it now, our separation has come about, I won't let you cover me again, I won't…"

She sat up a bit, and looked around.

"Where are you?" she cried. He was gone.

He had been in a hurry to start the second hand. Laughter could be heard from the next room. A mouse came out of its hole and began to scratch.

"So, I was speaking to myself," said Aglaia. "I am frightened." Another mouse appeared. Now they scuttled across the room. A water pipe must have broken, or else they were coming from the mines.

"I'm afraid," she said.

She hid her head under the quilt, pulling her hair down in front of her face. Hair was also a protection.

"Someday I must leave this region," said Aglaia. "I miss swimming in the open sea. 'View onto the Sea,' *Grigori* has written above his threshold. And even that is a lie. I am afraid. And Alexander's friend, who never understood, who doesn't suspect the tricks I played so that the postman would let me empty his satchel, nor even imagine what each second of separation has meant, each second of the twenty-four hours. My sister *Aglaia* is giving birth. What lucidity… good Lord, what supreme clarity. Our separation has been completed, I must tell it to you. I won't postpone it a moment. I will walk among the mice, right now, barefoot. I will step on them to come and tell you."

The hardest thing was to lift her head from under the covers, to tie her hair back in place on the nape of her neck. She looked toward the window. It was snowing. And from outside, a bliss suddenly came which ran through her spine, reached her heart and the tips of her fingers. One hand found and knew the other. They were the coolest shelter for her face. Her feet were warm despite the chilliness in the corridor—at least let nobody die, let nobody die ever—nor did she feel the least shudder when she opened the door and saw her husband and Dorothea in bed.

"Excuse me," she said. "I only came to say that our separation is now complete, that it is snowing outside and that I am no longer cold or afraid."

CHAPTER 9

Every mouthful we eat comes from the mines and has a metallic taste. We know it and know as well we haven't yet found the courage to say "as from today I stop living off the mines." It's precisely this Phokion blames us for—our hypocrisy. Though one must admit that Grigori hasn't sat regularly at the family table for years. There was no question of principle involved. Simply, he didn't have the time. Even after the war and his imprisonment, he ate wherever he happened to be and slept each night in a different house to avoid being trailed.

As for me, well, nobody bothers very much. In our times when you should be either sheep or goat, I am neither. I ravage my brains in order to decide, to say I am sheep or I am goat, yet I go astray. There must be something else, I tell myself, a metamorpho-

sis: let stones change and the essence of minerals.
Let me know *Alexander*, and let the fiancée love me
passionately. Meanwhile, I too live from the mines,
trying not to put on too much weight, and when
traveling, I go first class and always choose a hotel
with a view.

The rustle of the poplar tree on the river bank
reaches and enters the room; and all changes of
weather and the gestures of lovers are recorded in
the water. Before dawn you can cross the bridge and
go to the opposite bank or simply peer into the water
and see the exact moment light comes, the moment
when darkness becomes light. The other *Alexander*
goes perhaps only as far as the marshes. But I'm
sure he knows them well, he must cross them at
a run, without sinking in, he can spot each bird in
mid-air, quail or heron, and finally reach the beach.

And if you think of it, a lifetime is hardly enough
to know even our own district—unless you take the
asphalt road leading from Athens to the sea and the
ancient temple and move at sixty miles an hour.
Then two hours is enough, counting one hour at
my half-brother *Grigori's* tavern. And this is where
we legitimate children differ from the illegitimate
ones: we have certain advantages, and no matter
how sorry I may be for not knowing the marsh area
as thoroughly as they do, I would hardly have sacrificed my travels abroad, the arrival in a foreign city
where you should not mind if the railway station

coffee is too bitter. And when in the Alps, you shouldn't long for the sea. For if you climb over the mountain, you find another and another and still another peak, and you can go mad thinking that the sea is lost. Especially if you are anxiously waiting for a message from the fiancée.

Aglaia also believed she was going to receive a letter from my friend, despite there being little possibility of this. And every afternoon, she stood waiting out in the snow for the postman. He came at three or three-fifteen or three-thirty, but always suddenly: the village was boxed in and you saw him only at the moment he was taking his last turn.

As he was an excellent skier, immediately on turning, he was upon us. Aglaia, in her impatience for her letter, wanted to help him untie his skis, and he was offended that she didn't consider him swift enough. He used to say, "I won two first-place skiing prizes. You don't have any letters." Aglaia then insisted on seeing all the addresses.

"There might be a mistake," she said, and she emptied his leather satchel on the snow. She pretended to laugh at the combination of names, and she invented tricks in order to keep the postman a little longer. She formed sentences with the names beginning with the first or last envelope, and he laughed, but he also became annoyed for the ink on the letters smeared, and how was he to deliver them in such a condition? He'd put on his skis again and leave.

"Congratulations on the prizes," Aglaia would shout after him, "I'll have a letter tomorrow. It might even be at the post office now and have missed the delivery—or else it's still on the way."

She had become so reckless that she looked for my friend in movies or theatres at a time when each of them lived in a different city, half a continent apart. At the beginning of the performance she was always possessed by the same anxiety: she stooped forward to look around or turned behind in search of him; at intermission she paced up and down the aisle; during the second act, when the interest of the play was at its height, she examined each row systematically in her desire to catch sight of him; another intermission, and with the third act—the final disappointment that he was not in the hall at all. So why ever go to the theater, why travel, why search for him from city to city? She had become so desperate that one bright morning it occurred to her that he must be in the south; so she went to the south; no, he must be by the ocean, and she went to the ocean. For the same reason she crossed the Channel and went around London's suburbs; one of them she visited twice, with the hope that her first search had not been thorough.

"Always this longing of yours," Grigori had told me. "Who tells you that I don't yearn for things? In teaching the workers, do you think I enjoy upsetting the Old Testament idea of creation?"

Grigori was tormented by the knowledge that whatever he might say or do, he was born the legitimate son of a mine owner, he was raised on the mines—and that the other *Grigori*, despite his being a natural son and having every liberty, showed a disquieting behavior. It was rumored that he exploited the workers. He sold wine at a higher price than in the capital, and allowing credit was only a trick to make his clients drink more. Snacks were at astronomical prices. He said it cost him a lot of money to transport things out to this deserted spot. They also spoke about gasoline. How did he manage to have gas when nobody else did? Still, the main accusation lay in the fact that over the portal of his tavern he had written in huge capital letters "View onto the Sea." And this claim was not true. The sea could not be seen, save on unusually clear days. This falsehood might seem trifling to passing travelers, but to the miners it was of prime importance. Their longing actually made them believe they could see the sea. They read "View onto the Sea" and argued about its color, they could also see breakers and gulls when not even a breeze was blowing from the sea. Once there was a big row: somebody said he could see a ship, another saw a whole convoy, and they came to blows. In reality there were torrents of rain and no visibility whatsoever.

CHAPTER 10

The orders from Aristides Street had been clear.
Grigori was to set fire to the tavern two hours after
midnight. If the *owner* were to perish in flames
without so much as a cry, it would be all for the
best. If he were to try to escape, he was to let him
go, to avoid scandal, unless things were very quiet,
and then, in the utterly deserted night, he was to
fire one or two shots at him.

"Why the devil do they always have to choose
me for things like this?" Grigori mumbled to himself. "It's because they know I can handle things
well. Guaranteed success."

As the *foreman's* words were true and there was
proof of *Grigori's* guilt, he would hardly have
needed an order to burn up the scoundrel; but he
would have done it rather on a day and time of his

own choosing—not tonight when he would like to go ahead with his thesis, when a bright idea had come to him at the very moment the *foreman* was saying, "Phokion should be killed."

"You know the district better than anybody else," they told him. One of them said jokingly, "Aren't you the landlord's son?"

Eight men were gathered there. They asked why he was late.

"But were you expecting me?" Grigori asked.

"Of course, didn't the *foreman* let you know?"

"And I had the impression it was I who got him to talk," Grigori said. "I thought he had talked just by chance."

No, nothing ever happened by chance. The *foreman* had the mission of making him ask questions, of steering him to the point where, today, Grigori would force out answers in such a way as to cut the time-lapse between receiving orders and setting fire to the tavern—in the interim who knows what might happen?

Nevertheless, there was disagreement on just this point. Four of them said the job should take place two hours after midnight and four were for postponing it till the following night: things would be quieter then. Tonight was the union ball.

"The ball is out of doors," Grigori had said, "in the forest which the shepherds once set on fire. It would be better if we postponed action till tomorrow," he added—he was thinking of his thesis and the brilliant idea that he wanted to jot down.

They would have to consult with a higher official. Two of the dissenting party left for another address and the others waited. A woman appeared with a tray. She offered them *raki*. Orders were explicit: it was to be tonight, two hours after midnight.

"Fire lives the death of air and air lives the death of fire," Grigori said. "Goodbye. There won't be any snags. Just one match in the gasoline pump."

It was still early and he went to eat supper. Later he went somewhere else for coffee. Then another coffee.

When he arrived outside the tavern of the other *Grigori*, it was still early. He saw light and took cover on the far side of the road. Yet the stillness was unbroken.

Unexpectedly, the tavern door opened, and the owner, *Grigori*, stepped outside. It was then I approached and asked if the other *Alexander* had come by. Suddenly the gallop of the horse was heard, and… "Our sister *Aglaia* has given birth," announced the *rider*.

"*Alexander*," I was shouting after the *rider*, "*Alexander*, stop!"

And then it seemed to Grigori that the *owner* was completely drunk, for he talked loudly to himself, crying, "My *sister's* had a son, can't you hear, you beasts?"—although it was evident he was alone, Grigori concluded; there was not even the slightest indication of another voice. He spoke to the walls—and this wasn't the first time either—and sang, "We have killed God and we have many faces, we have killed God, we have lost our face."

"I'll teach you how many faces we have," muttered Grigori. "You won't have a single one left. As you fall asleep in your drunkenness, fire will devour you. It will eat your eyes, nose and your belly which is filled with wine. 'Fire will devour and judge you.' And Alexander, embittered by his desire, has found a good excuse to cover up his laziness and indifference. We're waiting for the miracle, but meanwhile we do nothing."

After the *owner* went back inside the tavern, Grigori climbed onto the road from his place of concealment.

"I heard you calling," Grigori said to me, as he approached. "The other day people saw you outside the fiancée's house, pacing up and down."

"I love her and I'm cold," I told him. "I want to return home to the fire."

"I'll come with you," said Grigori. "It's still early."

"You mean late."

"No, I mean early. I have time to tell you the story of the murder."

We didn't start drinking immediately, because, on opening the door, we found Aglaia unconscious at the foot of the staircase.

CHAPTER 11

I was back home with deep-seated bitterness, as always. I was still trying to guess the face of my brother called *Alexander*. Did he look like tree-shadows on the snow? If I had him in my two hands, I would tear him to pieces or slap him across the face. If only his horse were to slip and topple into a dark gully, if he were killed, then I would bend over him and wipe away the blood so I might see him. And I would kiss his forehead. If I had him in my two hands, I would tear him apart. The war between us was even blinder than the struggle between Phokion and the *foreman*, although they were fighting down in the mines.

Actually, I doubt whether Phokion knew whom he was dealing with. He saw the *foreman Phokion* daily and fought him inexorably. Their hatred swelled like a river in winter. The *foreman* wanted to get the upper hand, to take his place, he said, yet I doubt whether Phokion had recognized him as his illegitimate brother, or whether the question bothered him. For me, however, to know the other *Alexander* had become my whole life—and also to know my friend's fiancée. I wanted to seize her and kiss her on the hair, on the mouth, on the eyes, on the hair, on the feet, on the mouth, seize her and know her, and I couldn't do anything else but wander in the streets thinking of all this and imagining that I was kissing her hair, mouth, eyes, her hair, her feet, her hair, and telling myself that she must love me too, and at times believing it... telling myself she surely loves me since I love her; I was saying that she loves me though she had never seen me. Then I pondered how it was that my whole life had become this searching for the other *Alexander* and the fiancée. I could have chosen something easier—such as liking soccer or stamp-collecting or the girl who was afraid of bats. I roamed the streets thinking this affair might last for years, might never end; am I to stroll forever around the fiancée's home and the house of my other *brothers* and *sister*, seeing only undefined shadows?

After the war certain people said that pebbles gave them a feeling of disgust, as did all of life. A pebble doesn't give me any sense of disgust. Only I feel despair because it weighs in the palm of my hand as a foreign body, and I can't know whether it prefers sea-depths or the shore, sunlight or an overcast sky. I despair that everything stops at a certain point and that I may become ridiculous as I wait outside the fiancée's house, in such a central street where many acquaintances walk by. It would be humiliating if she were to see me, though she might understand how much I love her and she, at least, might tell me if she prefers sunlight or an overcast sky. There would be something perfect between us, without boundaries, a consolation for *Alexander's* attitude. The struggle with him tortures me more than the discord with my legitimate brothers, more than Phokion's deep contempt because I won't work in the mines, more than the irony of Grigori who says I'm indifferent to the world's destiny; yet during the war I displayed courage, I bombed and machine-gunned.

Grigori asks me whether I want the change to come, whether I believe in it. I tell him yes, but a radical change. Let everything change, down to stones and the substance of minerals.

I said to him, "Aren't I also to blame for your acts, for all the handgrenades you hurled and the powder fuses you set off under houses? Your ideas are mine, but you have distorted them. Why have you betrayed my ideas, Grigori?"

"You are responsible for my handgrenades," he answered me, sitting stiffly in his chair, "as I am for your bombs. Yet, with one reservation... I recognize that I destroy; and to help Nature in her task and her thirst, I want to destroy. Whereas you speak of fullness and other such absurdities. First you fight the other *Alexander* and then you want to be his friend."

"Grigori, why do you hang around outside the tavern every day? And tonight, while the *foreman* was dancing, why did your eyes fill with nostalgia as you looked out of the window?"

"I was thinking my distorted ideas," Grigori answered with irony.

"And also that no change came about in spite of all the grenades, did it?" I went on. "Before the war, the goals were clear, the line well defined. You knew where you stood, who was the enemy and who the friend, whereas now, well, it's all muddled. When you killed you knew why and you could belong to one party against another; now both play their hand at our expense, at the expense of our belief in change in the world. Foreign forces struggle, we are besieged from all sides and the circle tightens."

"Enough, Alexander, you're not saying anything new. And it's no solution to lie down with your eyes shut or walk about in the night. And by the way, when I found you a few minutes ago, whom were you looking for outside the tavern? I helped in preparing the party, but that's all I had to do with it. Then I went to a certain house on a certain street. Come, let's go in the other room where Aglaia is resting and have a drink and I'll tell you about the murder, in every detail."

The story seemed to prey on his mind, he always wanted to speak of it. This wasn't the only person he had killed, but this was the only man he had killed in such a manner. Before, it was on a battle-field, in the mountains or in the streets of Athens during the revolt—there were also the hostages on the forced marches, stragglers who would not keep up. But this victim was alone, going home.

"So listen," Grigori began, "he was alone…"

"Aglaia, do you feel any warmer?" I asked.

After finding her lying unconscious at the foot of the stairs, we had taken her into the living room where she was now cuddled up in an armchair near the fireplace. My friend had come and left again.

"Why do you trouble her dreams?" said Grigori. "Can't you see she's dozing?… Well," he continued, "he was alone and going home. Near the Reed River. A black night, fiendishly cold; a terrible wind. He had turned up his collar, his hands were in his pockets, his head lowered…"

Suddenly Grigori began to laugh.

"I told you all that to make it more dramatic," he said. "It wasn't cold and he hadn't turned up his collar. It was summertime, he was wearing a white shirt, and there was such heat and immobility in the air that you could even hear the buzzing of mosquitoes sailing out in swarms from reeds and green water. Look, Alexander, nobody ever attains fullness, not even Nature herself. The wheat ripens, but can it remain ripe? You either cut it down or it will rot. There is no fullness. There is only movement and change, a transformation of matter, destruction leading to renewal; and the secret is to identify yourself with this circular movement and aid Nature. We think we are satisfying our passions by fighting against each other; yet we satisfy only Nature, and still she never has enough of destruction. Man can never attain the magnificence of an earthquake or a volcano. That reminds me, Alexander, you never told me how it feels to bomb and machine-gun."

"Machine-gunning was interesting," I replied, "because we did it at a low altitude. The transformation of matter you speak of happens right in front of your eyes. It's no longer just an idea. You can see it. I also like night flying, because, then, searching for the fiancée and the other *Alexander* loses its importance; I mean, it is as if you knew them already, as if there were never any barriers."

"Hold on, Alexander, you're going astray. I asked you what it was like to bomb and machine-gun," Grigori reiterated. "I see you evade such subjects. Yet you have dropped bombs, and hit your target, too. You have bombed, and you can go on telling me about low flying and night flights or about the sun which suddenly rises as you fly in the high air and the harsh beauty of the world and other such literature. Yet you have bombed, you even dived to machine-gun—you saw men scuttling for cover and you picked them off. To your health, Alexander. Empty your glass. You've known the intoxication of destruction. We all tasted it: you in the air, I on the ground, Phokion under the earth. Phokion destroys without budging from the mines. 'The metal is used in war material of the highest quality.' To your health, Alexander. Drink it all down, and admit the intoxication of destruction, since you've tasted it. As for your conscience, re-member it is either God or Nature who wills these things: it is all part of their cycle. And don't forget our times. There is no limit to crime nowadays. Yet imagine, imagine if Nature were also to suffer from this movement and change that never reach fullness. You know, now I feel like bawling like a child... think of it, even Nature suffering. How would the suffering of Nature be? Would it involve pain? Alexander, I feel like crying."

I put aside the empty bottle between us and, reaching across the table with my two hands, I lifted his leaning head.

"What time is it?" Grigori asked me.

"You must have overworked yourself on this the-sis, you're all in," I said. "You have been used to other things these last years. You've been thinking of guns and ammunition."

"I must finish with Heraclitus before a new war comes," Grigori stated. "I want to have one thesis to my credit, in addition to the handgrenades. That's why I remain in this house and live off the mines. You see, first we became men and fought, now we must become adolescents and begin to study. Tell me what time it is."

"And we'll live this belated adolescence fully," I added laughing. "I feel very much like dancing tonight... to have many pretty women in a warm room, to dance with each one and hum *'Les enfants qui s'aiment'*, and not to think of the fiancée."

"What makes me and all our generation worthwhile," said Grigori, "is that we get ourselves killed for something bound to change: we believe in destruction and renewal. Not that we lack faith —we have much more than the fools of the past generation, the misers who expected payment and said 'Yes, I'll get myself killed, but for stable values and security.' We, we just give our lives away. Nobody promised us reward and security, but rather the opposite. We give our lives for change, or more exactly for one step in a greater change, knowing very well that this stage will also give way to another. After all, fullness and peace do not exist, and it is stupid to believe they ever will. I feel like crying my eyes out, Alexander. This generosity, my generation's giving away of everything. It's as if we suddenly drained ourselves of our blood. Yet I'm strong. You should have seen the rocks I broke when I was a prisoner; large boulders. But now we shall immerse ourselves in studying and finish our theses before another war comes… as of tomorrow, because tonight I have something else to attend to. I've just come from a certain house of a certain street and I have a task to complete before dawn. I feel like crying. Tell me the time, Alexander. Imagine if Nature suffered too…"

I leaned forward again and put my hand on his shoulder.

CHAPTER 12

"Aglaia," I cried.

"She's far away dreaming," said Grigori.

"Come out of it, Aglaia."

I rubbed her hands.

"Why don't you leave her alone, I've never been able to go into a faint."

"She's frozen. Who knows how long she was lying out there by the staircase in her nightgown before we found her?"

"And without her charming red slippers," Grigori said ironically. "Just look at her feet, her shoulders, her mouth. To tell the truth, I've never seen a more sensual creature than my sister. Even when she's out cold in a faint. If one gets to the bottom of all her tortured searchings and your anxieties, one finds that both of you think only of love. Look at her now, you could say that she's waiting for a man with every pore of her flesh. And if you lift her eyelids, you'll see the caresses she's dreaming of. I remember when she first became a woman and sat by the fire. I remember her look and the way she curled up like a cat. Would you tell me what you would do if somebody told you to go ahead and undress the fiancée, when you knew the other *Alexander* was just around the corner? See the angle of her hand. It's as if she were fondling a man's head, held against her belly, in order to postpone the moment and make the waiting last longer. Think of the sea, she says, and of the matings of fish, but I'm sure she feels sorry for fish because they can't know the act of penetration."

"Come to, Aglaia, and tell me if my friend has come."

"Yes, you think of penetration and not of the matings of fish. You can't fool me and won't prevent me from doing what I must. What is the time?"

"It is past midnight. Go bring some water and a woolen blanket. We may have to light the fire."

"I'll take care of the fire," said Grigori, "I like fireplaces and everything romantic: a sister fainting by the staircase because her husband was unfaithful or because her lover did not show up; a mother who has grown old without suspecting that her husband has baptized half the region—I say baptize to avoid using another term, and particularly since he was godfather to them as well—, a mother who has never seen the other house with the double fences."

"Have you actually met the other *Grigori?*" I asked anxiously.

"Every person has his own way of doing things. Our formal acquaintance will take place in a very few moments. But if you're asking me if I've ever seen him, I can say there was a time when I saw him every day. His tavern was our hangout and we drank wine together. Since then, the vineyards have dried up. This drought... Listen, Alexander, our family terrifies me. There are moments when I'm terror-stricken. When I think of this family, under each gallery, there is another gallery, and they are linked together in a maze-like pattern. Aglaia — Aglaia's husband—Dorothea—Phokion—the other *Aglaia*, and all possible combinations. Yes, the combinations are infinite and ambiguous, a picture in which it is impossible to tell subject from background—not because the drawing is undefined or the colors somber, but because the roles of subject and background can be interchanged; you do not know whom this outline belongs to, you see it one way, then another, my family strikes terror in me, which one of the two is Aglaia, who is...?"

"Quick, she's frozen."

I touched her forehead lightly.

"Snap out of it, Aglaia."

"Our *sister* has given birth," she said, opening her eyes. "It was a hard ordeal. Is it still snowing?"

"Yes, and you are extremely pale," I replied.

"I came close to her for the first time. Alexander, why do you walk so many miles? I have also been thinking that in London," Aglaia continued, "they had the clever idea of tearing down bombed houses. So in the city you see well-swept open lots. Cars are parked there, waiting for the theater play to be over, and the ghosts of air raid victims hear the first reactions to each performance."

"Aglaia, you're hiding something from me," I said. "I saw footprints on the stairs. Besides, I was expecting him."

"His footprints? Are you sure?"

She arose abruptly. Her face was illumined by a wild joy.

"Is it really true?"

"But what has come over you? Have you lost your mind?"

"There were so many forms coming towards me when I lost consciousness. Forms came and were perfect. I thought that too…The last clear thing in my mind was the sudden warmth coming from the window, and I said to them, 'I am no longer cold or afraid,' and then I felt hungry as when I was a child returning from a walk. I came down the staircase and… Alexander, did you really see his footprints? Are you telling the truth? He caressed my lips, now

I know it, my lips know it and will never forget it. I love his hands, I want to submit to his hands, I have been ready ever since this waiting for the postman – and night came quickly—I was embarrassed in front of the postman, I was swimming in the ocean because I said the sea is one, and it didn't matter if half a continent separated us, at that very minute he may have been looking at the sea; I have been ready ever since I bent over the river to watch the moment day would come for him, forgetting there was a whole hour's difference between the two countries; suddenly, over the bridge a cart came drawn by heavy work horses with heavy legs, and in it sat a little child with a red hood. Just think of that single red spot in the gray cart with the gray horses, a stark redness moving along a gray road of gray horses and gray pigeons, a flock of tamed pigeons…"

"So what happened?" I asked. I was wondering about the fiancée.

"He caressed my lips."

"Did you tell him about the postman?"

"No."

"And that you were searching for him from city to city?"

"I saw only his hands, two empty glasses and a ship painted on the floor, on the walls and the ceiling. We sat in the same armchair in order to leave space for the ships. He held me close, and still between us there was a whole plain, if I could cover it, I said to myself, if I could spread wings to cover it, if my blood were to become wings… Why should I have to speak and why doesn't he understand that I form everything according to his image, that I transform the landscapes so they will resemble him, that every object I see or touch is he, even the water I drink and the sensation of the glass in my palm? Nowadays horses have become so lean and the temperature of the earth has changed, streets are full of barricades, and cities are full of half-houses, 'your identity card please,' we are fed from the mines, we live off the mines, the metal of the mines is top grade, we make kitchen equipment and war material, 'Your identity card,' no trespassing, traveling is forbidden, no swimming off the beaches, can't you see the barbed wires?"

"If one could burn a whole village and then rebuild it stone by stone," said Grigori laughing. "Here is the blanket and the water. My sister, it doesn't take you long to recover and begin to chatter. Look how beautiful the kindling wood is. With it I shall light the fire to warm you and sweeten your love-dreams. Miserable times, really, when you can't swim with your lover, and lie naked on the sand with your eyes closed, waiting for him. You think of penetration and not of the matings of fishes. What time is it?"

"You will fill your heart with bitterness, Grigori."

"Come, my sister, let me look after you. I'll wrap you up in a blanket because your soul has frozen. I'll make you comfortable in this armchair which you love because he touched it, because the armchair is also he, isn't it? even the stool on which you rested your feet. Christ, what nonsense there is in the world! Now a bit of slumber. You know how to pass off into sleep and can afford to. Meanwhile, I'll finish telling Alexander the story of the murder. After that, all I'll have left to do will be to transplant the fire. Good, I see you have already closed your eyes; you're obedient." So, he was alone and going home...

...near the Reed River, the Reed River, the Reed River, the bullet surely must have hit him in the back, low flying is beautiful, she must ask Alexander whether he bombed the Reed River, but no, what silliness, one bombards enemy nations, she must remember to ask him through which nations he flew and the color of the children's hair. Airplanes buzz like mosquitoes, perhaps worse, yet Alexander did not bombard the Reed River, he could not have since the reeds were as high as mountains and low flying was impossible, since nobody passes there, even by foot, the bullets strike you in the back and while Alexander's friend was holding her by the hand, they were stopped by the police.

"Your identity card, please."

"I am Aglaia," she said.

"Your identity card."

"But I am Aglaia, don't you believe it?"

"We have no time to lose. The region is dangerous. Doesn't the word Reed River mean anything to you?"

"Where is your identity card, anyway?" Alexander's friend said, turning to her.

"Even you don't know me. I am Aglaia. Why don't you recognize me?"

"Your brother Grigori is guilty of murder," said the policeman. "Don't you see the dead man in the white shirt?"

"And your brother Alexander is guilty too," said another policeman. "He flew over the Reed River and machine-gunned."

"And your brother Phokion is guilty," said a third policeman. "He produces raw material for arms. There are even strange rumors that he supplies both sides. It seems that the Civil War is not unprofitable to him."

"Let me go," said Aglaia, "I haven't done anything. I don't even step out of my house."

"Then you too are guilty," said the third policeman. "How is it possible not to step out of one's house nowadays?"

"Yes, yes, I am guilty," said Aglaia. "Is this the Reed River?" She began to cry.

"But where is your identity card?" said Alexander's friend.

"Let me alone," she cried. "I have no identity card. Besides, I'm leaving this region, since you don't believe me either. I'll swim alone in the open sea. I have no identity card, leave me, I have no identity card, leave me, I have no identity card, I have no…"

"Aglaia," I said to her, "Wake up. It's nothing. Just a bad dream."

"We told you to slumber—not to shriek," Grigori said. "And if you have lost your identity card, I advise you to go tomorrow and have another one issued. Although I'm sure it slipped into the lining of your coat. Your pockets are always torn."

"The waiting begins again," said Aglaia. "The wind has risen and I did not notice the moment he left. I will become a statue on a promontory and I shall wait for him."

"The time is two o'clock in the morning," I said.

"I'm off," said Grigori. "My thesis will be extraordinary. Of course the professors are idiotic and won't understand it. 'You have to read at least forty studies on Heraclitus,' they will say to me. 'Why not a hundred?' I will answer, 'and what do you know about fire, about Nature that cannot reach fullness? It struggles and suffers, can you understand that?' Goodbye. I'm tired of your erotic fixations. They're the best excuse for stretching out by the fireplace or staying tucked up in bed on such a night as this. You are all hypocritical and you disgust me, you are hypocrites and guilty. You were not even capable of committing murder. Goodbye."

"Grigori!" shouted Aglaia, "Grigori! You'll only become bitter. Don't let him go," she implored me.

"Run after him."

"Grigori! Grigori!" I yelled after him.

He had disappeared. I didn't know which direction to take.

"The wind came up and my voice could not be heard," I said, on returning. "The desolation is immense."

"Yes," said Aglaia, "but I will keep trying. The unexpected bliss that came through the window to visit me, floods me with warmth and strength. I can embrace the whole range of the Alps and melt snow and glaciers from the peaks. One day this warmth will touch him, I know, but during this waiting, when someone knocks at the door, I fear my breathing may stop. And I fear lest *Aglaia* become distant again. She is beginning to recede, I feel it, Lord, don't let her go, let me keep this supreme lucidity forever, the memory of the first time I saw a bee and understood that the separation had been completed, now I am waiting for a knock at the door, for each knock could be he, couldn't it, Alexander? He caressed my lips, our *sister's* giving birth was a hard ordeal, Alexander, I have come to know our *sister*, as well as a transparency of landscapes, why should she fade away again? I want to know her more and more and I am waiting for a call at the door for each knock might be he."

CHAPTER 13

Perhaps Father laughs about this situation, and of course nothing seems strange to him. It is even possible that he arranged everything this way so as to be sure of amusing himself for the rest of his life. Whatever happens he doesn't reveal the least surprise. Yet recently, he has become more careful. A warning came from the marshes: there was a threat to kill him. One of the young women workers was pregnant. He must provide for her, they said, and in addition they demanded that he build a shelter for the women who work above ground, separating ore from the earth, because they were becoming consumptive. On rainy days the after-wind dried their wet clothes on their bodies. They threw old blankets or quilts over their shoulders, but this was worse, for the water seeped in and pierced them to the bone.

Nor was their hair enough protection. Water soaked through to their scalps and it was difficult for them to realize that they were cold. Their thoughts stopped, but what heaviness and rust, their heads hung as if full of old chunks of metal, knocking one against the other, old rusty iron from shipwrecked boats at the bottom of the sea. And their waists became warped. In their work they had to bend eight hours uninterruptedly, and at the close of the day they forgot to stand up straight again, and some of them no longer could. They warned him that they would kill him or blow up the mines.

This was not the first time the mines were in danger. There had been explosions in the galleries, and recently handgrenades were found hidden under fruit and vine leaves in a basket. One day the women threw their covers and quilts over their shoulders and stood below the windows of our house and cried:

"We want a shelter."

Then they remained mute. They made an effort to stand up straight, and cried again:

"We want a shelter."

The noise from the explosions was terrible. But the silence during the strikes was even more frightful; it spread below ground and expanded; it filled up space, and flooded like water which might have invaded the connecting galleries.

"If you had to cry for a shelter, there would be no more room for your longings," Grigori used to say. "Why don't you try to stay one day in the open air to separate the ore from the earth. It is a work full of interest and variety—to grasp this famous richness of the subsoil and imagine the life underground. Do roots of trees tremble on contact with the metal? The veins of metal must be solitary and tree roots are attracted away from them by sources of water. Metal veins are hard and break their way through rock, avoiding the soft flesh of the dead."

Father is unique in discovering veins of metal. He is proud of it, and is scornful of us. He is indifferent to everything, even to our discord. He would not blink an eye if you told him that Grigori excites the *foreman* against Phokion, or that the *foreman* arouses Grigori against the other *Grigori*, that the struggle has become general, without a moment's respite, since Grigori wars against Phokion, and Grigori and the *foreman* combat the other *Grigori* and Phokion. And I would tear the other *Alexander* limb from limb if I had him in my hands, unless I could kiss his forehead.

Aglaia dreams she is lost—in the mine galleries or in the corridors of the house—or that an object is falling from her hands and is also lost, that suddenly her door disappears and only half the room remains. The trees in the garden change place.

In her drive for a way out, she makes subterranean movements, but instead of coming out into the air, she finds herself in a lower gallery or at the point she started from—and still in quest of a way out or some kind of bearings.

The earth loses its balance, its relationship to the planets and its position in the firmament; there is a continuous falling, a dizziness and a sudden isolation within the dizziness where no one can come to your aid, because whether he puts out a hand toward you or supports your head, you are alone with the void; the earth disappears with all its crystals and precious stones, and bombing and new methods of destruction are but a detail when those who have escaped cremation lose their fingernails, their hair, eyes, virility, and women give birth to monsters or can never conceive again. The disappearance of cities is a detail when the earth strains to find its place in the universe, or find some point of support. A way out, you no longer ask for freedom; just to escape cremation or drowning in the gallery floods; and as you block underground currents of water or make them change their course, so you try to stop Grigori from combatting the other *Grigori* and Phokion; Phokion, Grigori and the *foreman*; the *foreman*, Phokion and the other *Grigori*; it is a labyrinth in which you lose yourself, but all this is only a microscopic detail since the earth itself is looking for a point of support in the abandoned world.

In our region, the vineyards go to rot. Even those that survived the bombs present strange symptoms, as if their trunks were hardened and assimilated into the metal. There is a fear that the wine will acquire a metallic taste, and so, then, even when drinking, the workers will not be able to forget the little ore-carts, the tuberculosis and dismemberment, nor the regular ease with which their wives conceive, nor the man who ten years afterwards was found crushed by a block of rock, whose flesh, instead of decomposing, had hardened into the metal.

At *Grigori's* tavern, they had begun to ask whether besides putting up the inscription "View onto the Sea," he didn't water the wine. No, he swore, it wasn't his fault. The vines had become crossbred, bastardized; at other times, he said, they had only to fear lightning and the impact of sun and stars, whereas now the influences were many and untoward. Unless it was the vines themselves that had worn out with age as was said of the mines and the quality of the ore, which was getting worse. Renewal was indispensable, new veins or a new mixture had to be found so that the metal might be regenerated and regain its first quality when it was born from the union of fire and earth. "The deeper we dig," Father says, "the fatter and stronger the veins become; perhaps one day we'll find the trunk." That's why in spite of the metal's inferior quality he doesn't stop digging, under each gallery a new one is opening up, the workers multiply and make fences of old tin cans around their houses. The Civil War flares. Foreign powers struggle and the ring tightens, towns do not know whom they should recognize as mayor, they are suddenly aflame, townhall and all, floors collapse, leaving window-openings completely blackened at night, and if two windows of the large hall happen to be in line, you can look through one window and see the opposite opening and the landscape beyond. Once the concern of the inhabitants was to endow the townhall with a big clock.

CHAPTER 14

"What are you doing here?"

Phokion jammed down on the brakes and snapped on the high beam.

In front of the iron gate stood the *foreman*. He was planted there with outstretched arms, barring entry.

"I came to see *Aglaia*. Move out of the way and open the inside gate so I can get through. And be quick about it. The motor won't run forever in this cold."

The *foreman* tried to step forward, but he tripped over his shoelaces, lost balance and would have fallen headlong onto the car lights if his trousers had not become entangled in the iron fence. He made some desperate gestures in empty space, and then straightened up, again spreading out his arms.

"No one passes here," he said. "In the hospital I couldn't stop you, but here it's my house. The wall and fence, the two doors are mine, I can slam them in your face if I want to."

"I must see *Aglaia*," said Phokion.

The *foreman* smiled. "You speak so firmly... as if you had every right."

"It was I who sent for the doctor and..."

"Yes, I know, you paid for the birth. And the doctor and everything down to the diapers. Of course the funeral, too, was done at your expense."

"What funeral?" whispered Phokion.

"Have you forgotten the accident in the mines and how *Aglaia's* husband was killed?"

"It was an accident," said Phokion. "I mean, it was a terrible accident."

"Terrible and inevitable," said the *foreman*.

"I see your tongue has loosened up," Phokion said, in a strangled voice. "At night you're no longer tongue-tied."

"I said inevitable. Who could enter a new gallery immediately after the explosion and come out alive?"

"The reward was immense," he muttered, "and there was a chance of escaping alive."

"I don't say it was not a well-paid-for death and a worthy funeral. Every honor for the person sacrificed in searching for new veins. In the heart of the earth, my godfather says, there grows a metal tree and we are looking for its branches—like children at play."

"Don't be ridiculous with your godfather. Get out of the way and open the inner gate."

"You're not coming in," the *foreman* shouted with all his strength.

Phokion pressed a button and all the car windows opened. It was freezing cold, but he had to be heard.

"I'm coming in," he cried, "even if I have to drive over you. I'll put on the radio to drown out your cries—if you'll have time to open your mouth."

The *foreman* posted himself before the door and began again to stretch out his arms, but then he preferred to cross them over his chest. He waited. Phokion turned a knob and the song *Les enfants qui s'aiment* blared forth. "The record Dorothea bought today," he thought. "I am married to Dorothea."

Then he stepped on the gas.

"You'll pay for this," yelled the *foreman*, who jumped clear at the last moment, scaling the fence like a monkey. "You'll pay for this and soon!"

CHAPTER 15

Phokion returned home to get his toothbrush. He would have liked to smash Dorothea's new record, and was annoyed to find it already broken.

"All this wasn't very clever of you," he said. "He'll lose his position in the mines."

"So that's what you were looking for," Dorothea cried. "You wanted to get rid of him."

"Of both him and you," Phokion whispered.

"You are cowardly and sly. You fear him as you do the *foreman*. You are frightened of everything, even your own shadow. But you'll see, your father will oppose a separation: Aglaia's husband gives him valuable legal advice."

"As of today, I'm going to set up my own house," said Phokion. "I've got my toothbrush and tomorrow I'm coming for the rest of my things."

"What solitude," said Dorothea, trying to put the bed in order. Suddenly, she sprang up and snatched the toothbrush from his hands.

"Don't go, Phokion."

"Give me my brush," he howled. He chased her around the room overturning the table, which in turn upset the chair. The cards fell in a jumble with her underwear and pieces of broken bottle.

"You'll never have a child and you don't feel the man inside you. Give me that toothbrush."

Her high heels caught in the underwear on the floor, but seeing the door open, she raced to the stairway, followed by Phokion. Once downstairs they tore open a door and came upon Aglaia and myself near the fire. They were both so embarrassed that he did not think of seizing the toothbrush, although he was very near her.

Yet at once he recovered his composure.

"A happy coincidence," he said. "I have certain things to announce to you. Let Grigori come too."

"Grigori went out to get some fresh air," I said.

"From now on," stated Phokion, "I am going to have my own house, I am going to demand my share in the mines from Father which I'll own and direct. I have a son," he said after a pause.

There were exclamations.

"Quiet," he said. "Don't play the innocent children—I can't stand this acting. Besides, how can anyone be surprised about anything that happens these days? Now listen to what I've got to say next."

Dorothea was on the point of fainting. They made her breathe in some vinegar. She was still holding the toothbrush and didn't know what attitude to take in front of Aglaia.

The latter, bending near her, whispered, "My hatred for you has diminished. We are all besieged, it is not your fault. Sit comfortably, and if you care to, lean your head back."

"I miss the ocean shore," said Dorothea, "and the turn in the road where you lose sight of the sea."

"I have a son," Phokion repeated. "I have a son from the *foreman's sister*."

There were more exclamations.

"Silence," he said. "I won't have any comments."

I began to say, "*Aglaia* is your…"

"I want no remarks, do you understand? How can anybody in our days be surprised about anything? This is my own life and my own affair. Here, I had no life of my own: on any night Father could wake me in the middle of my sleep and get me to repair his equipment. *Aglaia* has had a son. *Aglaia* has a round belly, and she has had a fat boy— my child. It weighs ten pounds. Call Father too. I have a few things to announce to him."

"It's not yet day," said Aglaia.

"Wake him up, we have no time. There is a threat of a general revolt and his life is in danger."

"Do not have any false hopes that they will cut my throat," Father said, after seating himself comfortably. "I shall live a long time, a very long time, I'll bury you all. Only when I am tired and have found all the veins I care to, will I curl up in a knot and die. But let's begin with the family. I hear there are some small irregularities. Aglaia, how could you decide to get a divorce without consulting me? Your husband is the best legal advisor we have ever had, he understands the work. We need him. At any rate his fault is not so terrible."

"Why yes, he hasn't even had a child out of wedlock," I put in.

"Don't interrupt," Father said. "We're coming to you."

He turned again to Aglaia.

"Did Alexander's friend come?" he asked.

"Yes," Aglaia said.

"Let him never set foot here again, do you hear? He makes all of you lose your head. This announcement of his engagement has swept you off your feet. You are imaginative and incapable. Not only can't you find metal, but you would not even know how to separate it from the earth, a job within reach of the stupidest woman."

"They are asking for a shelter," said Phokion.

"One thing at a time," Father said. "Do not interrupt. You are all good for nothing, I repeat, you like your comfort too. Alexander, from tomorrow, or rather in a few hours, since it is early dawn, you'll come with me to the mines. You'll begin to work."

"As of tomorrow, I begin to fly again. My application has been accepted."

"What are you saying? What's that?"

He pounded his fist on the table.

"So, everything happens without my knowing, does it? One of you is getting a divorce, another applies for…"

"And you haven't heard the pay-off," I murmured, smiling and looking towards Phokion.

"I want my share in the mines," Phokion said.

Father stifled a groan.

"You're all in it?" he said more loudly.

"I want my share—with a contract made up before a notary public," said Phokion. "I have a son."

"I know about your bastard child," said Father. "You have been feeding the *foreman's sister* very well all the time, and you've paid for the diapers the baby will piss into. But what has this to do with a share?"

"I shall live with her," said Phokion. "I'm going to set up my own home. I want a share, a share over which I'll have full command."

"Never," Father said. "The region belongs to me, every inch of it, down to the deepest gallery. And don't hope either for someone to come and butcher me."

"Your life is in danger," said Phokion. "I've already spoken to you about yesterday's committee meeting and their new demands. The cage cables are worn out and the *foreman* has insisted that they be changed immediately. You are in danger. The union ball was just a cover-up to hide those who tonight are plotting against you."

"As I was returning home," he continued, "there was light in the miners' cafe; it was closed, yet there was light inside. I saw two workers knock at the door and enter. Then four others. You don't go to a cafe for a drink at two o'clock in the morning. There is trouble in the air. I thought it was my duty to warn you. And if necessary, we'll protect you."

Father then laughed. In a flash, he recovered his strength.

"You—you good-for-nothings? You'd better look after your own skin first. If the mines were in your hands, Phokion, the miners would already have blown them up. I don't want to hear anything more about shares. Moreover, I have great plans for the mines; you will all benefit from them. That's why I also want Alexander with us. I have bought the land from our neighbor," he said in a low voice. "A real bargain. Alexander, during the war it was well and good to have an airman in the family; it added prestige. But now, we need someone of our own in the mines whom we can trust. I even find it humiliating to think of you transporting passengers and letters for a few pennies, like a bus driver, when you might instead be finding veins of metal…"

"I have made my decision," I said. "I shall no longer depend on you. I like the smell of airplanes and the special taste of the cigarette a few minutes before a flight."

"And no one will make me change my mind," Aglaia said.

"I want my share," said Phokion.

"So, it's a plot," shouted Father. "I'll…"

He did not have time to finish his phrase. Voices were heard in the distance. Phokion went pale.

"He's already wet his pants," Father said. "Look at the specimen who wants a share. Worthless good-for-nothing. You are all worse than those who are coming. You turn against me although we're of the same blood. You have your own ideas, have you? Yet you've been stuffing yourselves all these years, finding everything made-to-order. Not that I regret having worked like a dog; for it wasn't for you that I worked, but for myself, in order to find metal, for my own pride. It didn't bother me to throw out money so that Alexander could choose a good hotel, or Aglaia run from city to city in search of someone who didn't even suspect her love. I ought to have let you shift for yourselves, let you dig your own graves. You'd better know that if I take care of you, it's not for your sakes, but because I have a surplus of energy. Now open your eyes and ears and see how I'm going to handle them, how I'll twirl them around my finger and win. You thought I was going to wet my pants like Phokion, didn't you? That I would let them cut me up? You'll see."

The cries were becoming louder. One could begin to make out the words:

"A shelter, a shelter."

CHAPTER 16

Phokion's wife sleeps with Aglaia's husband, Grigori was thinking, Aglaia wants to sleep with Alexander's friend, Alexander with his friend's fiancée, and Phokion, faithful to tradition, sets up a line of bastards; but trying to outdo Father, he chooses for a mistress his own *sister*. Which family are they trying to preserve? Whom are they deceiving?

"Grigori! Grigori!" my voice trailed after him.

Grigori had to keep running. He heard me calling but he couldn't answer. He had a mission to perform.

"They claim I frighten them because I've killed men and blown up houses. But if they knew how they terrify me with the houses they are building and the children they bring into the world."

He stopped, picked up a handful of snow and rubbed his face.

"I shouldn't have been drinking and chattering away with Alexander. My head is heavy. What do I care if Aglaia was waiting for the postman? if Alexander lingers outside the fiancée's home and chases after the other *Alexander?*"

The snow did not refresh him. It set him more aflame.

"If I were not to kill him, perhaps I'd like to know him. No, I drank too much and my head is heavy, I don't care a hoot about such things. What I'm interested in is a crime as white as this snow. 'View onto the Sea' the rascal wrote, and in the cellar, instead of wine, he keeps arms and ammunition for the other side. I'll blow his skull to pieces along with the ammunitions; it will be a rare display of fireworks, gasoline mixed with wine, and the area will exhale stronger perfumes than the precincts of a lemon grove in spring. He must have made a deal with the foreigners: he gives them information in return for foodstuffs and gas and oil. In his shop, you're more likely to find Australian cheese than home-grown olives. And he has the nerve to say he wrote 'View onto the Sea' because it's the name of the tavern just as any other might be called 'Poseidon' or 'Friendship'."

"On Sundays, a band parades in the streets of Athens; the morale of the capital must be kept up. Was that Alexander still calling? No. Nobody was calling. Why doesn't Alexander call?"

The solitude was immense; in the distance shone the lights of the city.

"My head is so heavy, the battle is taking place in the streets of the capital. I am fighting from a third-story window, the house is surrounded and suddenly I discover there is no first or second floor, how will I get downstairs? How can I get out without a staircase or a first and second floor? I run onto the roof, impossible to leap over to the next house and hold out there, the houses have disappeared, the same with streets, squares, softly, without noise, as if they were made of cotton, it's no longer the capital and how will the band parade on Sundays, where will they pass? The musicians will scatter like jackals in the desert, and I'll run from roof to third-story window, from third-story window to roof and I'll scream…"

He had to hurry, it must have been two o'clock. The union ball was certainly over and his comrades would be together at the miners' cafe. This time they would not give way. Their first demand would be to have the pit-props which supported the layers of wet earth strengthened. As it was, at any moment they might collapse and bury them all alive. Then the cage cables. The cage grated as it descended, and as it became darker and darker and the lanterns lit up the streamlets of water on the wet-earth walls, one always had to be careful not to scrape one's foot or arm or shoulder. But now the danger was great, the cables were completely worn out.

On Sunday, the band parades in the streets, and in the afternoon when a breeze blows from the sea, you feel a deceiving calm. Why doesn't Aglaia have an identification card? He had three, one for any occasion.

"So this is where we were betrayed and caught like mice," Grigori said to himself, "where arms were hidden and watery wine sold at fantastic prices."

There was no wind, no snow falling when he arrived. A few clouds were passing before the moon and at odd seconds the lighting suddenly changed. The tavern was dark and quiet, the last light had gone out. The *owner* appeared to have tired of speaking to the walls; he must have sunk into sleep. He must be snoring away with a stinking breath.

Ten minutes to go. To be dead certain. The other *Grigori* had a habit of walking around outside the tavern at unusual hours—it was a pet delight, he said, he liked to get some fresh air and sober up. But who was he trying to kid now? He couldn't relax because of the arms-cache.

"I don't like these cloud-tricks. Here it's been dark and snowing all day and now the sky is filled with stars."

Yet it became dark again. The clouds thickened around the moon, white layers, then ashen and black.

He approached. The tavern lay above the level of the highway. From there you had a good view of the sharp turn and the accidents.

All at once the clouds scattered again and took another direction. The landscape was lighted. The roof gleamed white. And the nude branches of the fig tree, growing before the door, were whitened and silhouetted against the wall where the claim of a sea-view was written in large black letters. The asphalt road was stained with blood. Another accident. It was unlikely that a calf had been slaughtered in the middle of the highway.

He jumped into a ditch. In five minutes.

If there were a wedding taking place in the tavern… if the door were flung open, on the threshold you would see the newly-weds, bride in a white veil, groom with coal-black eyes. On the road they have killed and carved up two roosters for the wedding banquet. In the cellar are trunks filled with the embroidered trousseau. The music wafts up to the ancient temple. The young married girl looks toward the sea because she is still a maiden; the wind blows in from the sea. In the night, her lips will certainly taste of salt. On the highway, it's not even poultry blood, but red carnations.

Matches. If he had forgotten them… He reached into a pocket, then another pocket, crouching low in the ditch. In order for him to stand up, a cloud would have to cover the moon. Where were the matches? Ouhh! Got them. Yet the clouds were becoming thin; where in hell were they going? How small and white they became! In a while you might see well enough to sew—to embroider the bride's trousseau. He smiled. He always had peculiar ideas at such moments. The time had come. He had to crawl on his belly to reach the pump.

"I shall kiss her salty lips. Don't stare at the sea, turn your head towards me. I shall force her to turn her head. My eyes are black and you belong to me."

A match in the gasoline. Let everything become ashes. As things were, there was no choice. Only, he thought of those wooden tables which had just been painted green. The flame would leap up to the inside door; it might take the whole wall with it; running along the wooden floor, it would lick up the legs of the first table, the paint would crack, another table, and soon all the tables would be devoured by fire. If he could save those green tables, carry them on his back to the beach cafes where during summer a chill falls between couples when there is no table for the evening meal—silently they search everywhere—not to mention the pregnant women who cannot even find a chair on which to sit.

He had to finish with it. It was two o'clock. The revolver was in his pocket, ready for whatever might happen. If the *owner* escaped the fire, he would let go with one or two shots. He struck a match. The reservoir caught fire on the first try. The job was too easy. He almost missed the street-fighting. The day the big building was captured. A hard, beautiful battle. The reservoir was burning. The flames climbed the walls and the inside door. In a moment they would break through and enter the tavern. They would eat up the tables.

Again, he crawled across the road and dropped back into the ditch. From there he could watch everything without being seen. According to orders, he had to wait for the results.

"Why does this band of famished birds wheel above my head? My head has become heavy, where are the first and second floors? How shall I get down? Why are the streets and squares disappearing? Why is the region deserted? It's no longer the capital, you can't call a third floor without stairs a capital. Where are the neighboring houses? If I begin to holler from the window, who will hear me? How can I shout from the rooftop when all the city cats have rushed there and are piled up topsy-turvy in a heap? For cats are faithful to the cities; they do not disappear like men and streets.

No matter what the change, each city stays with its cats. How shall I get out of here? The flames are gutting forward, swallowing up the table legs and multiplying, spreading wider and higher."

"Help!"

Like the cry of a woman giving birth in the desert, a cry filling the whole desert.

"Help!"

"Help!"

The desert is peopled with women giving birth, the flames encircle the tavern, all sides are blocked, the wooden door is aflame, how can you get out, which way out, for the love of God a way out to escape cremation and spare your eyes and hair. Those who are dead drunk do not understand, perhaps they will understand at the last moment when the flames reach their eyelashes, the panic-stricken rush to the inside door and are reduced to ashes, others run like mice between the green tables, stepping over the drunks, trampling on their faces, somebody jumps into the flames and opens the door, they rush outside, there is a breeze, the women's hair is flames riding the wind, they try to put them out but their hands catch fire, their dresses are also in flames and how can they take them off when their hands are burning, help! only a few manage to come out, they scream, a dog howls, then all the dogs of the neighborhood, the cocks crow, a woman holds a dead child in her arms, and on the borders there are children who are out of their minds, who recognize neither their mothers nor the stairway of their homes.

"Help! Help!" Grigori cried. "Help! Who can escape fire? Help! Help!"

He ran along the road all the way to the ancient temple at Sounion.

CHAPTER 17

A band of famished birds. If the snow did not melt today, they would fold their wings high in mid-air and drop earthwards. Birds also become heavy. Or they dream of plains sprinkled with grains of wheat after harvest time. They flew round and round, tracing insistent circles as if, shut up in a room, they were searching desperately for a window. You might have said that their wings scraped against the walls. The low sky was of a uniformly ashen color, and with a great weight pressing down, you did not know whether the birds came from high up or whether they sprang from the earth.

"A shelter, we want a shelter."

When will the days begin to get longer? The women had thrown blankets and quilts over their shoulders. Their shoes were heavy with mud. If this winter would only finish. Or if at least death would come peacefully so that a house or a street might return to its calm. So there might be no more steps and threatening voices. One cannot even find milk for the children nowadays.

The men had hung their mining lanterns from their caps. They carried placards on which was written: "Higher Wages," "Safety Measures." But they only shouted: "The cables!" And the women: "A shelter! A shelter!" Finally a third group appeared crying: "Death!" And on their placards was written "Death."

The birds became numerous. They flew low and shrieked. They came from all directions.

"A shelter! A shelter!"

"The cables!"

"Death! Death!"

Someone brought out a revolver and fired into the air. The birds scattered at once. And suddenly a bullet cracked through the dining room window and buried itself in the wall.

"Hide yourself," said Father. "Go and get my coat so I won't catch cold. I'm going out on the balcony."

We tried to hold him back.

"Out of my way," he said. "You've lost your heads. Quick, my coat. I'm coughing."

Mother did not understand. All she did was repeat, "No, no, no!"

"My coat, I'm telling you," Father cried.

They had reached the front door below. And as their shouting increased, one could no longer make out separate words: one group did not wait for another and their voices mixed together in a booming clamor.

"Death! A shelter! The cables!"

They were howling.

Then Father suddenly went out on the balcony. The surprise was great. There was a hush. They lifted their heads to see. Dawn was beginning to break.

"I'm asking for only five minutes," said Father. "You are right about everything."

He waited. The surprise continued. They were paralyzed.

"I have something extremely pleasant to announce to you. But before I go on, I must explain a few things. First, I want to ask you—do you think I don't suffer, too? Do you think I don't see that your wages are too meager, that we lack equipment and an efficient system of lighting and ventilation? But, as you know, the means don't exist. Our country is poor and mining is expensive. We have greater costs than any other nation, and yet we are forced to sell metal at their prices. And so our profits are next-to-nothing or nothing at all. If wages went up, my costs would exceed the market price and I'd have to close down the mines; do you understand that? I would close them and you'd be without bread. It's the same for improvements. Improvements require spending, enormous spending, my costs would again exceed the market price. I have spent whole sleepless nights looking for a solution. It's not my fault, you must know, it's destiny. But now destiny has changed. I have something extraordinary to announce to you. I have found a vein of gold."

"Gold! Gold!"

"Gold! Gold!"

"Gold!"

"Gold!"

"Naturally, a very thin vein. But it must begin somewhere, it must thicken and unite with other veins. We will find many veins of gold. Why shouldn't we find many? We shall find the source of the gold veins. We'll dig deeper, we'll open new galleries. We will dig, won't we?"

"Yes, yes, we will dig."

"Gold!"

"We will go deeper, even to the center of the earth—isn't that so?"

"Yes, we will dig."

"We will dig."

"Gold!"

"Gold!"

"Better wages," cried another.

Shots were heard. A bullet grazed Father's head and dug into the shutter.

"The cage cables," a third man shouted.

"A shelter," the women cried out.

"The cables will be changed tomorrow," Father yelled as loud as he could. "I will also take care of the bracings and the shelter. But be patient about wages. Now that I have found the vein, everything is going to change. By spring perhaps, you will all be rich—did I say rich? I mean very rich. By spring. I have found a vein of gold do you hear that?"

"Gold!"

"Gold!"

"Gold! Gold!"

Father reached into his pocket. Then he stretched out his open palm.

"I've got gold dust here," he said. "From the gold vein. Do you want to see it?"

"Yes! Yes!"

"Gold!"

"Gold!"

Without changing his position, he opened his fingers very slightly. The gold dust spread onto the snow. They rushed from all sides, one on top of another, ready to fight with each other. They were digging in the snow. They were still clamoring, but for a different reason.

"Silence," Father said. "I haven't finished. I have more good news. We have a double hope. Not only have I found this vein, but I am experimenting in order to turn metal into gold, whatever metal we find will become gold. I know my new laboratory has excited your curiosity and imagination," Father smiled. "There have been many rumors concerning it. Not only among you, but everybody, even my own children. Now I'll tell you what the new laboratory is for. Why do you think I shut myself up for hours? I am studying the ways of transmuting base ores into gold. One day I shall find it. I am positive. And everything will change, there will be no more cause for war, there will be a basic renewal, all will change I tell you. Hope for it with me, shout as loud as you can 'Everything will change.' In my most recent experiment... But why should I bore you with all this? I work for you, I work hard, I rise before the sun and I am the last to sleep. While others waste time talking, I bury myself in study, I don't know what rest means— or pleasure trips, or dancing. All that I care for is a glass of wine, I like what you like, don't you see we're alike? Now go. Today let's begin work an hour ahead of time in order to inaugurate the new era. By spring everything will change. Be patient. All will be different. We will find many veins. We will find the source of the gold."

"Gold!"

"Gold!"

"Gold!"

"Now about-face and go."

He shut the balcony door and came back inside.

He stood behind the curtain until he saw them turn and leave. Then he asked for coffee and a chair for his legs.

"Father, have you really found a vein of gold?"

"I do not want coffee, I prefer camomile," he said.

"Won't anybody move? I said camomile."

"Have you really found gold?"

"There is nothing I've got to account for to any of you. You are going to pay dearly for your conspiracy."

"One way or another, I want my share," said Phokion. "Right now I'm going to make a survey down to the deepest gallery, and decide on a way of making the division."

"The region belongs to me," Father roared. "I won't let you touch a stone of it. And the fact is, Phokion, I don't see what you have to complain about. I've provided your wife with furs and perfumes. And you two," turning to Aglaia and me— meanwhile Phokion had slammed the door behind him—"you've never missed going on trips. As for Grigori, I have never understood what he wanted. One day he asks for enormous sums of money and the next he throws them back in my face." Here Father grinned. "One night I was tying sheet strips together so he could shimmy down from the back window because they were after him—and she," pointing to Mother, "was trembling like a leaf. 'Why isn't there any rope in the house?' I asked. She was trembling as if it were the first time…"

"But where is Grigori? Where is my son? Are they after him again?"

He turned to Mother.

"Do we have any rope in the house?"

"He didn't sleep at home," I said.

Mother was pacing up and down. She had lost her equanimity and was saying, "No, no, no."

"It must be some woman," chuckled Father. And he started to pace up and down, anxiously.

The workers had already disappeared from in front of the house. They were walking along, taciturn, their heads lowered. For a moment the women said, "A shelter, we want a shelter," they said it from habit, as if speaking to themselves. The birds followed, flying lower and lower. The snow became black slush weighing down their feet. The same road every day.

"Supposing we all become rich," someone interjected.

They were fooled. There was always a way to fool them. Yet there was a hope, and after all something might happen to change everything. They had heard about mines where, unexpectedly, gold was discovered and the place became rich, and the girls, instead of sifting metal ore from earth, tied their hair with real silk ribbons, a different color each day, and paraded along the waterfront. As for the metal becoming gold, why should one exclude even that; so many things happened nowadays; in a second one can annihilate a whole city, however big, and trips to the moon are not far off.

"By spring, our pockets will be bursting with gold," said another, with a bitter laugh.

CHAPTER 18

"So my *sister* is your mistress, the baby comes from your seed. It wasn't enough for us to be bastards, our children had to be, too. I detest you, Phokion. You even stole my name. They christened us both Phokion and I'm left with the name '*foreman*.' Last night you humiliated me in front of my own door. If you'd gone a little further, those car wheels would have ripped out my insides, while the radio was blaring away. But now you'll taste death in the cage. You didn't want the cables changed, huh? You talked of studying the question as part of the budget. You'll understand the budget and how one's ribs can be smashed from a height of twelve hundred feet. Your flesh will become hashed meat. If I could see your flesh the second it is crushed, if I could be inside your flesh to see it. You have held me down

ever since I remember, every day, as with a medicine
dropper. Now I am going to put you down, once and
for all. You've nearly driven me mad with anger. I'm
going to crush your ribs. Everyone knows the cables
are worn through. But even if they suspect I've
helped them along with a few flicks of my knife,
nobody will breathe a word. Every one of them will
welcome such an accident. You'll go like a special
delivery parcel to the deepest gallery, and if you
have a few breaths left, the gas will finish you off.
Yes, there is gas, Phokion, in the deepest gallery,
you know it, only yesterday you refused to pay overtime for clearing it up. You also know it's impossible
for us to take time out from our regular work without
falling short of the inspector's quota. Then they'd
even cut our daily wage. Let an explosion take place,
I don't care, you thought, is that it? Let them choke.
Let them spit blood. Well, it's you who are going to
spit out your last breath."

"Are you speaking to yourself now?" Phokion
said, approaching. "Or is it the cage you're addressing? Move aside. I'm going to visit the deepest
gallery. I must determine the share I'm going to ask
for. Hurry and find the fitter, and have him meet me
below."

"Do you have anything else to say?"

"Yes, I love your *sister* passionately."

The *foreman* stood aside and Phokion waited
before the cage.

"We're agreed about the cables. Have them changed. Meanwhile, don't let more than two at a time go down. When there's no great weight, there's no danger."

"Right," said the *foreman*.

"Look at them. Today they work differently," said Phokion smiling. "Because of the gold." Then he turned to the *foreman* and looked straight into his eyes. "I love your *sister* passionately."

And he entered the cage.

CHAPTER 19

Phokion was killed.

They are looking for Grigori. Two disfigured women, without hair or eyelashes, came to testify that they had seen him, it was definitely he they saw jump out of the ditch. He called for help and ran towards the sea. The police and the families of those who were burned are pursuing him. They are searching the coast, they are closing in from all sides. Before evening he will be taken.

It was for them that he wanted to struggle, to fight in the streets, but he burned them instead and now they are pursuing him. It won't be an outdoor prison this time, and he won't be able to make his escape by swimming.

In the house of my other *brothers* and *sister*, there had been light throughout the night in the north room. *Aglaia's* cries could be heard. The *foreman* was shouting, "No one passes here." Then people came to bring news of the fire.

All has been devastated and reduced to a pile of cinders. The tavern which used to separate the mines from the fields is no longer there, neither is its *owner* (he became ashes), nor the "View onto the Sea." The scene where the road sharply curved has changed and you come upon women with seared eyelashes and without hair. Grigori is being pursued. He will also pay for my bombing and machine-gunning, for my stretching out at high noon with shut eyes, for Aglaia who is guilty because she didn't do anything: we've put the whole load on Grigori's shoulders and by evening he will be caught.

I linger by the house of my other *brothers* and *sister*. When they light the north room, I can't tear myself away, I shout—as Grigori from the third floor, yet nobody heard him—I shout to *Alexander* that it would be good to go to the ancient temple in April without being pursued. And it is a pleasure to sit in a waterfront cafe when they're not pursuing you. During the day two ships arrive, they unload livestock and phonograph machines; you are never bored. And perhaps the fiancée will arrive. Yes, there she is: first she'll wave to me from the deck —white becomes her and she'll be dressed in white—she will descend the gangplank, my God! how long it takes her to come down the plank, she will touch land with her gaze riveted to me, and come and give me her hand.

"So, you have doubted?" she will say to me. "You shouldn't have."

"I never doubted," I shall tell her.

Aglaia doesn't doubt either. A moment will come, she says, when she will lift her eyes to see my friend looking at her ardently. He will have guessed about her going from city to city in her quest, to the ocean and that accursed London suburb. She waits for him to knock at the door and how often does she turn down a street and tremble—is he at the corner? No, but surely he is at the next corner. He will look at her fervently, and so that not a thing will separate them, they will tell each other what landscapes they have known, how many ports and Sundays.

Standing before the other house I shout up to the window where I suppose *Alexander* to be that it is beautiful everywhere if you are not pursued and that we have strength, even too much, but to what end? We are praying for a way out and some kind of bearings. Shall we always wander with the same longing?

"We heard her screams from here," said Aglaia, looking up at the north window. "Tell me if you see her, tell me quickly."

"My friend could see her when she was undoing her hair," I said.

"I am waiting for him from moment to moment."

Suddenly she became extremely pale. She was looking fixedly at the north window and was very pale.

"*Alexander* has left," she said, "and will never come back. He left at dawn with the fiancée."

I turned around and looked at her.

"I must run and catch up with them," I cried. "Aglaia, goodbye," I said, caressing her hair, and I rushed to the airport.

MODERN
GREEK
CLASSICS

C.P. CAVAFY
Selected Poems   BILINGUAL EDITION
Translated by David Connolly

Cavafy is by far the most translated and well-known Greek poet internationally. Whether his subject matter is historical, philosophical or sensual, Cavafy's unique poetic voice is always recognizable by its ironical, suave, witty and world-weary tones.

STRATIS DOUKAS
A Prisoner of War's Story
Translated by Petro Alexiou
With an afterword by Dimitris Tziovas

Smyrna, 1922: A young Anatolian Greek is taken prisoner at the end of the Greek–Turkish War. A classic tale of survival in a time of nationalist conflict, *A Prisoner of War's Story* is a beautifully crafted and pithy narrative. Affirming the common humanity of peoples, it earns its place among Europe's finest anti-war literature of the post-WWI period.

ODYSSEUS ELYTIS
1979 NOBEL PRIZE FOR LITERATURE
In the Name of Luminosity and Transparency
With an Introduction by Dimitris Daskalopoulos

The poetry of Odysseus Elytis owes as much to the ancients and Byzantium as to the surrealists of the 1930s, bringing romantic modernism and structural experimentation to Greece. Collected here are the two speeches Elytis gave on his acceptance of the 1979 Nobel Prize for Literature.

NIKOS ENGONOPOULOS
Cafés and Comets After Midnight
and Other Poems   BILINGUAL EDITION
Translated by David Connolly

Derided for his innovative and, at the time, often incomprehensible modernist experiments, Engonopoulos is today regarded as one of the most original artists of his generation. In both his painting and poetry, he created a peculiarly Greek surrealism, a blending of the Dionysian and Apollonian.

M. KARAGATSIS
The Great Chimera
Translated by Patricia Barbeito

A psychological portrait of a young French woman, Marina, who marries a sailor and moves to the island of Syros. Her fate grows entwined with that of the boats and when economic downturn arrives, it brings passion, life and death in its wake.

STELIOS KOULOGLOU
Never Go to the Post Office Alone
Translated by Joshua Barley

A foreign correspondent in Moscow queues at the city's central post office one morning in 1989, waiting to send a fax to his newspaper in New York. With the Soviet Union collapsing and the Berlin Wall about to fall, this moment of history would change the world, and his life, forever.

ANDREAS LASKARATOS
Reflections
BILINGUAL EDITION
Translated by Simon Darragh

Andreas Laskaratos was a writer and poet, a social thinker and, in many ways, a controversialist. His *Reflections* sets out, in a series of calm, clear and pithy aphorisms, his uncompromising and finely reasoned beliefs on morality, justice, personal conduct, power, tradition, religion and government.

ALEXANDROS PAPADIAMANDIS
Fey Folk
Translated by David Connolly

Alexandros Papadiamandis holds a special place in the history of Modern Greek letters, but also in the heart of the ordinary reader. *Fey Folk* follows the humble lives of quaint, simple-hearted folk living in accordance with centuries-old traditions, described here with both reverence and humour.

ALEXANDROS RANGAVIS
The Notary
Translated by Simon Darragh

A mystery set on the island of Cephalonia, this classic work of Rangavis is an iconic tale of suspense and intrigue, love and murder. *The Notary* is Modern Greek literature's contribution to the tradition of early crime fiction, alongside E.T.A. Hoffman, Edgar Allan Poe and Wilkie Collins.

EMMANUEL ROÏDES
Pope Joan
Translated by David Connolly

This satirical novel and masterpiece of modern Greek literature retells the legend of a female pope as a disguised criticism of the Orthodox Church of the nineteenth century. It was a bestseller across Europe at its time and the controversy it provoked led to the swift excommunication of its author.

ANTONIS SAMARAKIS
The Flaw
Translated by Simon Darragh

A man is seized from his afternoon drink at the Cafe Sport by two agents of the Regime by car toward Special Branch Headquarters, and the interrogation that undoubtedly awaits him there. Part thriller and part political satire, *The Flaw* has been translated into more than thirty languages.

GEORGE SEFERIS
1979 NOBEL PRIZE FOR LITERATURE
Novel and Other Poems   BILINGUAL EDITION
Translated by Roderick Beaton

Often compared during his lifetime to T.S. Eliot, Seferis is noted for his spare, laconic, dense and allusive verse. Seferis better than any other writer expresses the dilemma experienced by his countrymen then and now: how to be at once Greek and modern.

MAKIS TSITAS
God is My Witness
Translated by Joshua Barley

A hilariously funny and achingly sad portrait of Greek society during the crisis years, as told by a lovable anti-hero. Fifty-year-old Chrysovalantis, who has recently lost his job and struggles with declining health, sets out to tell the story of his life, roaming the streets of Athens on Christmas Eve.

ILIAS VENEZIS
Serenity
Translated by Joshua Barley

The novel follows the journey of a group of Greek refugees from Asia Minor who settle in a village near Athens. It details the hatred of war, the love of nature that surrounds them, the hostility of their new neighbours and eventually their adaptation to a new life.

GEORGIOS VIZYENOS
Thracian Tales
Translated by Peter Mackridge

These short stories bring to life Vizyenos' native Thrace. Through masterful psychological portayals, each story keeps the reader in suspense to the very end: Where did Yorgis' grandfather travel on his only journey? What was Yorgis' mother's sin? Who was responsible for his brother's murder?

GEORGIOS VIZYENOS
Moskov Selim
Translated by Peter Mackridge

A novella by Georgios Vizyenos, one of Greece's best-loved writers, set in Thrace during the time of the Russo-Turkish War, whose outcome would decide the future of southeastern Europe. *Moskov Selim* is a moving tale of kinship, despite the gulf of nationality and religion.

NIKIFOROS VRETTAKOS
Selected Poems   BILINGUAL EDITION
Translated by David Connolly

The poems of Vrettakos are rooted in the Greek landscape and coloured by the Greek light, yet their themes and sentiment are ecumenical. His poetry offers a vision of the paradise that the world could be, but it is also imbued with an awareness of the abyss that the world threatens to become.

AN ANTHOLOGY
Greek Folk Songs   BILINGUAL EDITION
Translated by Joshua Barley

The Greek folk songs were passed down from generation to generation in a centuries-long oral tradition, lasting until the present. Written down at the start of the nineteenth century, they became the first works of modern Greek poetry, playing an important role in forming the country's modern language and literature.

Rebetika: Songs   BILINGUAL EDITION
from the Old Greek Underworld

Translated by Katharine Butterworth & Sara Schneider

The songs in this book are a sampling of the urban folk songs of Greece during the first half of the twentieth century. Often compared to American blues, rebetika songs are the creative expression of people living a marginal and often underworld existence on the fringes of established society.

AN ANTHOLOGY
Greek Folk Tales

Translated by Alexander Zaphiriou

Greek folk tales, as recounted throughout Greek-speaking regions, span the centuries from early antiquity up to our times. These are wondrous, whimsical stories about doughty youths and frightful monsters, resourceful maidens and animals gifted with human speech, and they capture the temperament and ethos of the Greek folk psyche.